Eli B. Toresen

Dangerous Summer II

Part 1:
What The Forest Was Hiding

Copyright: Text © 2006 by Eli B. Toresen
Published by PONY, Stabenfeldt Inc.
Cover photos: Fotograf Kallen
Cover layout: Stabenfeldt A/S
Translated by Osa K. Bondhus
Typeset by Roberta L. Melzl
Edited by Bobbie Chase
Printed in Germany 2006

ISBN 1-933343-19-2

Chapter 1

"Just admit it, you're in love with Justin!"

Heather looked up with a start. She had been so absorbed by the task of combing out tangles in Caliban's mane that she hadn't noticed that somebody had entered the stall. She saw the teasing look in her best friend Angelica's eyes.

"I'm not!" Heather tried to make her voice sound convincing, but her face was blushing treacherously, saying differently.

"Ha! You don't fool me for a second!" Angelica laughed. "Why do you even bother to deny it? If I were you..."

"I know, if it had been you, you would have walked right up to him and asked him out." Heather gave a sigh. "But I'm not you."

Angelica shook her head impatiently. "You're shy to a fault, Heather. That's your problem. If you wait too long, somebody will eventually snatch him right before your eyes. You're not the only girl in the stable who'd like to get closer to Justin, you know. I might just walk off with him myself, if you don't get your act together and do something about it."

Heather stiffened. Angelica saw her reaction, and chuckled. "Just kidding! You know that I have my eye on someone else right now. Just too bad he's on vacation and will be gone the entire summer. But maybe it's just as well, because this way I'll have more time to hang around here with the horses."

Heather was about to say something, but just then Betty walked into the stable, and they didn't talk about Justin anymore.

"Hi, Angelica!" she called cheerfully, with a friendly nod toward Heather. "I'm glad you're still here. I thought you might have gone for a ride. There's something I'd like to talk to you about, if you have time to step into my clutter zone for a moment."

Heather looked at Angelica and Betty as they headed toward the office at the other end of the building. Betty wasn't exactly Mrs. Organized when it came to papers and such, hence she often referred to her office as her "clutter zone" or the "messy room."

Betty Madison had been the owner and manager of Stardust Stable for two years now. The stable had been in a deplorable state of neglect when she took over, but in no time at all she had renovated the buildings and made the place look great. However, the main reason the stable had turned into such a popular riding school was because of Betty's personality, Heather thought to herself. You couldn't find a more energetic and inspiring riding instructor. At least not that Heather had ever met before. She was so happy she had been able to board her horse at this particular stable.

Heather looked at Caliban, who was patiently and peacefully standing by, nibbling on some hay. She still had to pinch herself sometimes, to make sure that this gorgeous horse actually was hers. All hers, from head to toe. Her thoughts wandered back to her thirteenth birthday, about a year ago. She hadn't had the slightest expectation that she might get a horse. Of course she had been wishing for a horse for many years, but her parents had always said she'd just have to be patient and wait. If she was still interested in horses when she got to be 14 or 15, then maybe...

Therefore it had been a total surprise when they gave her the card revealing the most fantastic gift in the world. She had opened the envelope expecting to find a gift certificate for a CD or maybe some riding pants. Instead she found a big colorful postcard with a picture of a beautiful, white Arabian horse. The card read:

Dear Heather,
Happy Birthday!
We can't promise you the horse in this picture, but if you come with us tomorrow, we'll introduce you to Caliban. He's a six-year-old Swedish Warmblood, bay with white blaze, and he's yours if you want him. No need to worry about where you'll keep him. We've talked to Betty Madison at Stardust Stable, and he can be boarded there.
We hope you like your gift!
Love, Mom and Dad

Heather still remembered the tingle of excitement and anticipation she had felt as they drove to the stable where she would see Caliban for the first time. Her feelings had been mixed with a certain degree of anxiety as well, because what if it turned into a fiasco? What if Caliban didn't like her? What if she didn't like Caliban?

She tried not to worry. And it was love at first sight, at least on her part. Fortunately it seemed like Caliban accepted her too. Not that there hadn't been a few breaking-in problems. Caliban was a strong-willed horse. There's no telling how things would have turned out had it not been for Betty. She had been a great support, giving useful advice and tips on how to handle him when he refused to budge. Now, a year later, she and her horse were completely on the same wavelength. Heather trusted Caliban and he felt safe around her.

She stroked Caliban across the bridge of his nose and scratched his forehead. He loved to be scratched and cuddled, and gave a loud, contented snort.

"You're the prettiest horse in the world. And of course you know that already, even without me telling you all the time." Heather ruffled his mane as she glanced at her watch. How long was this going to take? She and Angelica had agreed to go for a long ride in the nice weather, to celebrate the start of their

7

summer vacation. But it was beginning to look like Angelica had taken root inside Betty's office. Could something be wrong, perhaps? Nah. If so, Betty wouldn't have looked so cheerful, she thought.

One after another, riders were finishing up their preparations and leading their horses outside. Some were taking lessons, while others were just going for a ride. Heather chatted with some of the girls as they went by while she waited, becoming increasingly impatient for Angelica to show up. She also had a secret wish that Justin would be here today, but the stall where his horse usually stood had already been empty when Heather arrived that morning. He must have gone for a ride at the crack of dawn.

Justin had been coming to the stable for only about a month. He and his mother had moved here from a nearby town. Justin's mother was an old friend of Betty's, so naturally his horse, Bogart, was boarded at Betty's stable. Heather had been totally impressed with Bogart when she first saw him. He was a large, powerful black Friesian horse with a long, flowing mane. She hadn't really paid much attention to Justin at first, but after a while her heart began to throb every time she saw him. He was two years older than she, tall and slender, with the bluest eyes you ever saw. Justin seemed friendly enough, but there was no indication that Heather's growing feelings for him were mutual. *It'll probably never happen either,* she thought pessimistically. *Nobody else is as idiotically shy as I am when it comes to guys.*

She envied Angelica, who was the most outgoing person Heather had ever known. Angelica didn't seem to have the slightest trouble finding something to talk about, no matter who she was talking to. Heather, on the other hand, couldn't count all the times she had desperately been racking her brains for something to say, while her mind just felt blank and empty, unable to come up with any good ideas. She was okay as long as the topic of conversation was horses, but if it went on to other things, then she was in trouble. Especially if she was talking to people she didn't know very well. And she hadn't known Justin for very long at this point. She probably wouldn't get to know him either, if she was just going to stand around blushing with her mouth open like a fish out of water every time he said hi.

Heather sighed and tried to focus on being careful as she put Caliban's saddle on his back. He was touchy about certain things, and having the saddle dumped on his back too abruptly was one of them. If that happened, he could be irritable and moody for hours afterwards.

Finally, she heard a door opening and closing, and Angelica came sprinting toward her. Her face was flushed with utter excitement.

"You won't believe this!" she yelled, startling Caliban and making him jump and throw his head back as if to say, "What's the big commotion?"

"What? Tell me! You look like you've been sitting in a pressure cooker or something, and you almost scared my horse to death, so I assume it's something totally sensational!"

"You bet your boots!" Angelica was so excited she was practically jumping up and down. "You remember Crissy, the horse that was boarded here for a while last year?"

Heather nodded. Crissy was a beautiful, dapple full-blooded filly with a spunky temper. Angelica had sometimes helped Anna, Crissy's owner, with her training.

Angelica flailed her arms around in a totally animated state. If she had been a bird, she would have taken flight, Heather thought as she stifled a giggle.

"Anna is going to France to study for a year. Crissy is going to be boarded here, but Anna doesn't want her to be used as a school horse because of her temper. Betty wants me to groom and ride her while Anna is gone! Apparently Anna had asked

9

for me, because she remembered me having such a good handle on Crissy the times when I was helping her. Just imagine, a whole year! It'll be just like having my own horse! Yippee!"

Angelica started dancing down the hallway so fast, she stumbled on her own legs and almost fell over. It looked so wildly amusing, Heather had to laugh. And Angelica laughed along with her. She was in bubbling spirits, which Heather could easily relate to.

Heather had often felt a bit guilty because she was the lucky one who owned the world's most wonderful horse, while Angelica, outside the riding lessons she was paying for, had to be content with whichever horse Betty let her borrow. Not that there was anything wrong with those horses, but it wasn't quite the same when she had to switch from horse to horse all the time, depending on whichever one was available. But Angelica didn't have much of a choice.

Her mom was a teacher with a modest income. She and Angelica had been alone since Angelica's dad died in an accident when Angelica was only two years old. Angelica barely remembered him at all, and therefore didn't really miss him, but now and then she would think about how things might have been different if he had lived. They would probably have had more money, and her mom might have been happier and less worried. And best of all, she might have been able to have her own horse. Every time she thought like that, though, she felt guilty. Her mom had done the best she could, and it wasn't her fault that things were the way they were.

In return for borrowing a horse, Angelica worked a few hours at the stable, helping Betty with whatever she needed help with. But even if Betty was so nice and willing to let her borrow a horse, there were times when Angelica couldn't have one, simply because they were all being used for lessons. That's why Angelica welcomed the news about Crissy as if she had won the jackpot in a lottery.

"I think this must be the best day of my entire life!" she exclaimed dramatically. "Is this going to be a fantastic summer, or is this going to be a fantastic summer?"

"Without a doubt, a fantastic summer," laughed Heather. "Are you riding Gilbert today?"

Angelica nodded. Her face was still one big smile from ear to ear.

"Well, could you go and get him ready then? We'll be retired citizens before we get out of here!"

A little later, as Heather was leading Caliban out of the stable, she was blissfully unaware of the creepy and horrifying waking nightmare she would soon get sucked into.

Chapter 2

"This is the good life!" Angelica was lying in a comfortable sprawl on the grass, looking up at a few fluffy white clouds drifting across a vivid blue sky.

Heather didn't answer. She was lying almost in a daze, peering at the horses which were tethered each to their own tree. They were grazing peacefully, clearly without a worry in the world. Heather's thoughts went from the horses to the one person she had been thinking the most about lately – Justin. She started daydreaming that Justin was the person lying next to her in the grass. They had gotten back from a fantastic ride together, and Justin had just told her that he had been in love with her from the very first time he saw her. "You have the most beautiful eyes I've ever seen," he said tenderly, looking at her with his intensely blue eyes. "And your smile..."

"Earth to Heather!" Angelica's voice brutally interrupted her dream. Heather reluctantly sat up and looked at her friend.

"Were you sleeping?" asked Angelica.

"No, I was just thinking about something..." To her dismay she felt herself blushing again. Fortunately Angelica didn't seem to notice.

"What were you saying?" Heather yawned and stretched.

"I was just saying that we'd better get going."

Heather nodded, got up, and walked over to Caliban. He greeted her with a low neigh, as if he was saying, "Are we going already? Can't you see I'm doing something important? I'm eating!"

Heather smiled and ruffled his mane. "Do you know what a

food monger you are? Be glad I ride you every day, or you'd be as fat as a barrel by now!"

Caliban shook his head and nabbed a juicy tuft of grass. The thought of becoming overweight didn't seem to worry him in the slightest.

Heather and Angelica had just gotten in the saddle when they heard neighing from somewhere in the woods. Apparently there were other riders nearby.

Maybe it's Justin, Heather caught herself thinking. She hadn't even finished the thought before horse and rider came out where she could see them. And sure enough, it was Justin. He was riding through the woods at a breakneck speed, as if he were running from a police troop on a stolen horse.

"Has he lost his mind?" Angelica said in shock. "Riding at a speed like that outside of the trail and everything! What if Bogart stumbled over a root or stepped into a hole?"

Heather didn't answer, but she was just as shocked as Angelica at the reckless way Justin was urging his horse on. She would never have believed this about him.

Angelica tried to wave at Justin as he thundered past the clearing where the girls were sitting on their horses. But Justin was staring straight ahead with an expression of stifled anger on his face. After he was gone, the girls looked at each other. Angelica's face was red with fury.

"I'd like to report him to Betty," she said. "I've never seen such reckless riding!"

Heather didn't know what to say. She was on the verge of tears from disappointment. Here she had walked around thinking Justin was such a kind and sensitive boy who was fond of his horse, and then he treated Bogart like that.

"Maybe we should talk to Justin before we say anything to Betty?" she finally said, quietly.

Angelica thought about it for a second and agreed. "But he's

13

going to hear what I think about his riding," she said in a war-like tone of voice.

When the girls rode their horses back onto the trail, Angelica discovered to her dismay that one of Gilbert's front shoes was getting loose. After checking it carefully, she determined that she couldn't continue riding with it. She patted Gilbert on the neck with a sigh.

"I'll have to lead him home on foot. No point in taking any chances. Betty wouldn't like it if I came home with a limping horse."

She turned Gilbert around looking at Heather over her shoulder. "Are you coming with me, or what?"

Heather thought for a second. "You go on ahead. I'd like to ride over to the Linden pond really quick, then I'll come right back. Bet I'll catch up with you long before you're home."

"Okay." Angelica shrugged her shoulders and started walking.

"See you in a little while." Heather got Caliban in motion along the trail. A mild breeze ruffled the treetops, and the sound of chirping birds filled the air. She gave a sigh of well-being. Could life get any better than this? Her mind drifted to Justin for a moment, as she thought about the way he had ridden like a madman through the woods. Then she forced herself to think of other things. She was not going to let Justin's reckless riding ruin her day.

A squirrel caught her eye as it effortlessly climbed up a tree trunk. She watched the little reddish brown animal running along one of the branches, taking off for a leap, then gliding through the air and landing on a branch in the neighboring tree. Imagine being able to climb trees like that. It must be a great feeling. Heather smiled while trying to imagine herself jumping from branch to branch, steering with the help of a bushy tail. It was such an amusing thought, she had to laugh. But suddenly she stopped. She had heard a sound that didn't belong in here between the trees and the chirping of birds.

14

There it was again, the sound of scraping followed by a thud. More scraping and another thud. It sounded just like somebody digging. But who would be digging here, deep in the woods? Heather got curious and started riding in the direction of the sound. There, in a small clearing between the trees, she saw a car. An unusual sight, she thought. Heather couldn't ever remember having seen cars in this area before. She could also see the back of a man. He raised his back and lowered it again in a jerking motion, and when he turned his body a little, she saw that he had a shovel in his hands. Her curiosity grew. The soft forest ground dampened the sound of Caliban's steps, so Heather was almost at the clearing before the man suddenly discovered her.

He straightened up with a startled expression. "Hey, what the..."

Heather didn't hear the rest of what he said. Her gaze had caught sight of something lying on the ground behind the man. It was an oblong package, nearly six feet long maybe, wrapped in dark gray plastic. The shape reminded her of, of...

Heather felt the terror shoot through her as she realized what she was actually seeing. A man digging a large, oblong hole in the ground, and, and...

Oh no, this couldn't be true. Surely she must be hallucinating. That couldn't be a person lying there on the ground, wrapped inside the gray plastic. Because if that was a person, then that would mean...

Heather's hand was clasped to her throat to squelch a scream building inside her. But except for that motion, she couldn't move. It was as if she were in a video after someone had pushed the pause button and frozen the picture. She could barely breathe from sheer fright.

Then there was a movement in the corner of her eye. The man. Apparently he had momentarily frozen to the spot just like Heather. But now he was coming toward her, lifting the shovel in the air.

The movement broke Heather's paralyzed state. With a gasp she dug her heels into Caliban's sides and pulled hard on the left rein. Caliban turned obediently toward the left and started trotting.

Heather heard a roar behind her and turned her head. The man had thrown the shovel aside and came crashing through the brush that was the only thing separating him from Heather and Caliban. In a moment he would be through the brush, and then...

In total panic, Heather drove Caliban into a gallop. He stretched out, seemingly happy for the opportunity to run. Heather clung to the saddle while dodging a branch that came dangerously close to her head. Was he coming after her? She didn't dare turn around to look.

Her heart was beating so hard she could hear it resounding in her head. Her ears were buzzing, and black dots danced before her eyes. She felt like she was going to faint. No, that mustn't happen! She tried not to think about the man now, or the terrible thing she had just seen. She must concentrate on staying in the saddle. Heather clenched her teeth as she leaned forward. The trees were rushing past her like indefinable shadows. Then she saw the trail, the wide, familiar riding trail. Heather gave Caliban free reins. Some place up ahead was Angelica, Gilbert, and safety. If she could just get to Angelica or the stable, she would be safe. She still didn't dare turn around. Logic told her that the man could not possibly run so fast that he could keep up with a horse in full gallop, but fright had gotten such a hold on her that logic didn't help much.

It seemed like an eternity before she caught sight of two familiar figures, Angelica and Gilbert. She felt an enormous relief. But just as she was about to holler for Angelica, she thought she heard the sound of a car. The sound came from some place ahead of her. The man! He must have taken a shortcut in order to cut her off! Heather suddenly felt nauseous, and her head

16

felt kind of light. She pulled the reins as hard as she could and opened her mouth to scream. Was there any sound coming out? She didn't know. The trees, sky, and the trail, everything started spinning around her, faster and faster. She could tell that she was sliding sideways in the saddle. Then everything went dark.

Chapter 3

"Heather? Heather?! Talk to me, Heather! Wake up! Can you hear me?"

"Hmm?" Heather heard Angelica's voice. It sounded like it came from far away. Why was Angelica making so much noise? Didn't she understand that Heather just wanted to be left alone, to keep sleeping?

But Angelica kept on shaking her and shouting her name. Reluctantly Heather opened her eyes. She caught a glimpse of some trees and a blue sky. What was this? Why was she lying in the woods sleeping? Then she remembered. She and Angelica had gone for a ride in the woods. But when had she lain down and gone to sleep? She and Angelica had parted for a while, she remembered that quite clearly. But afterward...?

Suddenly it all came back to her. She sat up so suddenly that Angelica, who was squatting next to her, rolled over with the sudden movement. It felt like the ground was moving underneath her and she felt very nauseated, but she couldn't worry about that now.

The man! The man who had followed her, where was he?

Heather looked around with a wild look in her eyes.

"Heather! What's the matter with you?" Angelica had gotten up and was sitting on the ground. "You scared me to death almost. First you came riding toward me so fast I thought you had a monster on your heels, and next thing I knew you fainted and fell off the horse. Good thing I caught you before you hit the ground. What happened? It's not like you to ride like a madman!"

"Did you see anybody else? A man, a car? I mean, a man in a car or maybe he was on foot?"

Angelica stared at her friend without comprehension.

"What are you going on about? Did you hit your head? Do you have a concussion? How could a man in a car be walking? And exactly what man are you talking about? Did somebody scare you? A man?"

Heather nodded, looking faint. Her eyes were still searching the surroundings as if she expected someone to jump out of the bushes at any moment and attack her. What if he was nearby, maybe behind that tree, or over there?

Angelica said something, but Heather didn't catch it. She pulled herself together and focused her attention on her friend again. When she finally heard what Angelica was saying, she shook her head vigorously. That wasn't a smart thing to do, because a wave of nausea washed over her. She moaned and bent her head down between her legs. That's when she realized that her riding helmet was lying on the ground next to her. Angelica must have taken it off while she was unconscious.

She looked up at Angelica. "No, nobody tried to kill me," she said. "I think I saw a... a murder!"

Angelica's eyes widened with shock.

"Well, not the actual murder, that is." Heather tried desperately to collect her thoughts. Then she told her friend what had happened as best she could.

"No wonder you fainted!" said Angelica when she finished. "May I borrow your cell phone, please?"

"Huh?" Heather looked confusedly at Angelica. Here she was, talking about her life's worst experience, and all her friend cared about was her cell phone?

"What do you want that for?"

"To call the police, of course." Angelica rolled her eyes at her stupid question. "We should call the police, don't you think?"

Heather stared at Angelica, befuddled. Of course. Why hadn't she thought about that? She had been so scared she hadn't thought of anything else but getting out of there as fast as she could. She was still scared, even though it felt a little safer now that Angelica was with her. Her gaze went toward the woods again. Everything seemed quiet and peaceful. No sign of anybody else around, and even so she felt like eyes were watching her from the trees.

"Heather! Honestly!" Angelica sounded irritated.

Heather turned around and looked at her. Angelica handed the phone back to her. She didn't understand at first; did Angelica want *her* to call the police? But then she saw it.

"Oh no!" she sighed. "I forgot to charge it last night. The battery is dead."

"We'll just have to ride to the stable and call from there," said Angelica. "Can you manage to get up on Caliban, do you think?"

Heather nodded and scrambled to her feet somewhat unsteadily. The sooner she got away from the woods, the better. She put her helmet back on and walked over to Caliban. Angelica had tethered him and Gilbert to some bushes nearby. Heather stroked him across the bridge of his nose. "You were great!" she said. "You may actually have saved my life. There's no telling what that man would have done if he had caught me." Caliban snorted calmly and shook his head, making his mane dance. Heather checked the girth and swung into the saddle.

Angelica did the same on Gilbert. "We're not that far from the stable," she said, "so I'll just risk it and hope the shoe stays on until we get there. C'mon, let's get out of here!"

Heather wasn't going to argue. She urged Caliban into motion as she resisted the temptation to turn and look behind her. There's nobody behind me, she told herself. Even so, she felt a prickly feeling down her spine, as if someone was staring at her.

Betty reacted quickly when Heather and Angelica arrived at the stable and told her what had happened. She called the police, who said they would want Heather to show them the place where she had seen the man bury the body. Heather felt nauseated by the mere thought of it. It hadn't occurred to her that she would have to go back to that place. Betty offered to go with her, which Heather gratefully accepted.

"I should call your parents too," said Betty while they were waiting for the police to arrive.

"Is that necessary? My dad is overseas on a business trip, and my mom is at the office. They can't do anything about it right now anyway." Heather's eyes pleaded with Betty. "My mom has so many problems at the office right now. The last thing she needs is another thing to worry about. Maybe she doesn't need to find out at all," said Heather, sounding hopeful.

"Oh, I think she does. We can't keep a serious thing like this from your mom. I'm sure you understand that. But of course I could wait until after you've shown the police where you saw the man digging." Betty followed Heather into the stable.

Heather led Caliban to his stall, took the saddle and bridle off of him and put on his halter. He had stripes of sweat in his hair, making her feel guilty for having ridden him so hard. But she knew it had been necessary. And fortunately it had ended well.

Heather was surprised to see that her hands were shaking when she started brushing Caliban. Betty saw it too. "It must be the after-effect of the shock," she said. Then, to distract Heather, she started chatting in a friendly tone; "You mentioned that your mom has problems at work. What kind of problems? Or would you rather not talk about it?"

"Oh, I can talk about it," said Heather. "It doesn't really have anything to do with my mom, personally, I mean. But the company she works for is apparently involved in some shady affairs. Something about corruption and bribery. You've probably read about it in the papers."

21

Betty nodded. "Yes, I read something about that the other day, but I had no idea that your mom works there. The director of the company is apparently in a lot of trouble, if I remember correctly?"

"Mm-hm," the police went to his office and confiscated papers, and a bunch of auditors are apparently going through all the accounting. My mom said he didn't come to work yesterday. Heather stretched to reach the top of the mane and started detangling Caliban's mane. He closed his eyes and seemed to enjoy the attention.

"No wonder your mom is worried," said Betty. "Maybe you should give her the same treatment you're giving Caliban and see if it's just as relaxing for her as for him." She smiled as she looked at the horse standing there looking totally blissful.

"That's an idea." Heather giggled.

Just then they heard a car pull up outside.

"That must be the police," said Betty. Heather suddenly felt a tight knot in her stomach. For a few minutes she had almost managed to forget the frightening scene she had witnessed earlier. But now it all came back to her again. With a sigh, she gathered up her grooming tools and carried them into the saddle room.

"Good luck!" shouted Angelica from Gilbert's stall.

"Thanks, I think I'll need that." Heather hesitated for a moment inside the stable door. Then she straightened her shoulders, took a deep breath, and went outside to meet the police officers. Outside she also saw Justin, who had just gotten on his bike, ready to head home. He said hi and she gave an automatic and absent-minded answer. For once, his presence didn't make her heart throb. All of her thoughts were focused on the ordeal she was faced with.

Chapter 4

"I don't understand this!" said Heather for the umpteenth time, as she looked at the trash bag lying on the ground in front of the police officers.

One of them gave a sigh of resignation. "Well, I think it's pretty clear," he said with a touch of irritation in his voice. "Your imagination played a trick on you, that's all."

"But this is not the bag, or the package rather, that I saw." Heather looked stubbornly at the police officers.

They just shrugged their shoulders and didn't answer.

Heather had not been watching as they dug up the plastic bag. She didn't want to see what it contained. Not until one of the police officers exclaimed, "What the... What's the meaning of this?" Then she turned around. Instead of the oblong plastic package she had expected to see, the police had uncovered an ordinary trash bag filled with empty beer bottles and an old sweat suit with paint stains.

Heather couldn't believe what she saw. What had happened?

"Are you sure this is the right spot?" The oldest of the police officers gave Heather a searching look.

She nodded. "I'm completely sure," she said. –"The man who was digging ran toward me through the bushes over there." She pointed. "You can see where a lot of the smaller branches are broken. I'm a hundred percent sure that this is the right spot."

The police officer nodded. "But you can see for yourself that the reason for the digging was far more innocent than what you thought."

At this point Betty stepped in. She had stood by quietly, listening to what they were saying, but she could no longer keep silent.

"Don't you find it a little peculiar that someone would bother to drive way into the woods just to bury some empty bottles and a sweat suit? I mean, why wouldn't they just recycle the bottles and throw the sweat suit in the trash? I think that's really strange."

The officer shrugged his shoulders again. Heather was beginning to hate this motion.

"There are a lot of peculiar people around," said the youngest of them. "This one must have been more than a little strange, if it's true that he acted threatening."

"He must have," said Betty firmly. "Heather is not easily scared, and I have never seen any evidence that she has a particularly wild imagination. You should therefore assume that the man acted the way she says he did."

Heather felt a warm gratitude toward Betty for the way she was standing up for her, though it didn't seem to make much of an impression on the policemen. They took the bag and put it in the trunk of the car, slammed it shut, and motioned for Heather and Betty to get in. Nobody said anything on the way back. Heather felt her anger grow into a fury when she stood outside the stable a little later, watching the police car driving away in a cloud of dust. When she couldn't see it any longer, she turned to go into the stable. She noticed that Betty gave her a searching look. Heather felt her cheeks get warm. Betty didn't say anything, but Heather had an unpleasant feeling that deep down, Betty too must think that the body in the bag only existed in her imagination.

Her stomach churned as she recalled the conversation in the car on the way out to the woods. The police had asked her what the man had looked like. Heather had started out just fine.

"He was medium tall and a medium build," she had told them. "He was dressed in khakis and a brown sweater. He had

24

brown hair. His face was... his face." She stopped, somewhat bewildered. She had seen the man face to face. But when she tried to recall his face, she saw only a cloud. She simply couldn't remember what the man looked like. And she hadn't been able to say anything sensible about the car he had been driving either, other than it being a regular passenger car in some neutral color.

Hence all she had given the police was a bag of trash and a fumbling description of a man without a face. No wonder they had had problems believing her story.

While still standing outside the stable, she had again tried to conjure up a picture of the man's face, but to no avail. The more she tried, the less she remembered.

But he will surely remember you! said a little voice inside her. A cold shudder of fright shot through Heather. She threw a glance over her shoulder as if she expected the faceless man to be standing right behind her. Nobody was there, of course. Heather shook her head and hurried into the stable. Inside the stable, among all the familiar smells and sounds, she could feel the fright let go of her. She felt safe in here.

The following day Heather had to endure lots of more or less funny comments about the discovery of the trash bag. Angelica was the one who had slipped the news about what had happened. Heather couldn't really be mad at her for leaking it, because Angelica was the only one who really supported Heather and completely believed what she was saying. The others around the stable seemed to just think the whole thing was amusing.

"Hi, Heather," said a dark-haired girl named Elizabeth as she passed Caliban's stall carrying some empty bottles. "I'm just going outside to get rid of these bodies! Unless you'd rather bury them in the woods for me, ha, ha!"

Heather stuck her tongue out behind the girl's back, but it didn't make her feel any better.

25

"If I get one more question about having any new leads on the 'empty bottle murderer,' I'm going to lose it!" hissed Heather when Angelica joined her in the stall later that morning. "Not to mention the jokes about 'the faceless murderer'."

"I am so sorry," said Angelica remorsefully. "If I'd known how this was going to turn out, I would never have said a word to anybody! But since I had already told everyone that you went to the woods with the police to show them where the murderer had buried his victim, I didn't see how I could not tell them what they found."

"And then you just had to tell them that I didn't remember what the man looked like. No wonder people think I'm a complete dork!" Heather sighed, and started scratching Caliban behind the ears. He snorted quietly and blew a cloud of warm breath mixed with half eaten straws of hay toward her throat.

"Hey, you rascal! This sweater was clean this morning!" Heather held up a threatening fist toward him, but had to laugh when she saw the innocent, bewildered look in his eyes.

"By the way, what did your mom say?" asked Angelica curiously. "You told her what happened, didn't you?"

Heather nodded. "Yeah, I promised Betty I would tell her. Otherwise I don't think I would have. Actually, I'm not sure she heard much of what I said anyway. She said 'gosh' and 'you poor thing' and things like that in the right places, but sounded pretty distant, really."

"Worried about her job?"

Heather nodded again. "Her boss didn't show up yesterday either. The audit staff tried to get hold of him, but all they got was his answering machine. Mom thinks it's only a question of time before they arrest him, and then the company may have to shut down completely. If that happens, my mom loses her job."

Angelica opened her mouth to say something, but before she got a chance, they were interrupted by Justin who came up behind them. "Hi! So this is where you guys are hiding."

Heather turned around and felt the familiar quickening of her heartbeat again. Her mouth felt totally dry as she looked into Justin's blue eyes.

"We're not hiding," said Angelica quickly. "I thought maybe you were, though. I haven't seen you since yesterday."

"You saw me yesterday?" Justin sounded surprised. "I can't remember seeing you. I said hi to Heather outside the stable, but..."

"No, you didn't see me," interrupted Angelica. "But Heather and I certainly saw you! You should be ashamed, riding your horse the way you did! That was totally crazy and irresponsible!"

Heather suddenly realized that she had totally forgotten Justin's wild riding the day before. So much had happened since then. And besides, Heather had ridden at least as wildly herself, so who was she to criticize Justin?

But he rode like a madman for fun, while you were fleeing in a panic, said her inner voice defensively. *There's a big difference between the two.*

Heather suppressed the irritating voice inside her. She didn't want to think badly of Justin.

She looked over at Angelica, who stood in front of him with her hands firmly on her hips and an accusing look on her face.

Justin was red in the face and looked like he wished he were a thousand miles away.

"I... I didn't think anybody had seen me," he said numbly.

"As if that would make it any better!" Angelica shook her head. "What if your horse had been injured? Didn't you think about that?"

Justin shook his head. "No, I didn't really worry about that right then," he said. "But I agree with you, it's not very smart to ride that fast in the woods. I'll keep that in mind."

"You'd better," said Angelica as she walked toward one of the empty stalls. Crissy would be arriving the next morning, and

27

Angelica was anxious to get everything ready for her dream horse.

Justin went into Caliban's stall and started scratching his forehead. "You had quite a ride too, I've heard." He glanced over at Heather, who blushed and felt ill at ease.

"I guess everybody has heard that story," she said, looking down. "I know what I saw, but the police don't believe me, so there isn't much I can do about it."

"What about the man you saw? You still don't remember what he looks like?"

Heather shook her head. "His face is like a cloud in my mind. It seems like the more I try to remember it, the foggier it gets." She giggled nervously, but mentally she gave herself a big kick in the shins. Why was she standing here giggling like a silly little girl? Why did she always act so awkward and stupid around Justin? Why couldn't she just talk to him in a natural way?

"I think you should just stop trying to remember," said Justin as he scratched Caliban's mane. Caliban shook his head contentedly, as if he was saying, "Ah, that feels good! More, please!"

Heather looked at Justin with surprise. Surely, it must be important for her to remember what the man looked like.

Evidently Justin understood what she was thinking. He leaned toward her. His voice was low and urgent. "Sometimes it's better to forget things. Better... and safer!"

Before Heather could say anything, he left the stall and disappeared down the stable hallway.

Heather was left looking thoughtfully at him as he left. That was a strange thing to say. Did Justin mean to say that she was in danger? If so, it must mean that he also believed she was telling the truth about what she saw. The thought made her feel warm at first, but then the feeling changed to a chill down her back. A horrible thought just occurred to her. If she didn't remember what the man looked like, he could walk right past her in the street without her knowing it. And he could follow her, to the stable or to her home, without her being able to recognize him.

Heather cast an anxious glance about her. The cozy, familiar stable, which up until now had seemed so warm and safe, suddenly felt foreign and scary.

Chapter 5

"I'm so excited, I can't stand it!" Angelica paced back and forth in the stable hallway, all in a fluster. "If the horse trailer doesn't show up soon, I'll go raving mad!"

"Sounds like you already are," commented Heather. She had just walked into the stable after having taken a loaded wheelbarrow with wet stall bedding out to the muck pile.

Heather rubbed her eyes with the back of her hand. They felt like they were full of sand. She hadn't slept very well that night. At first she had been lying awake for the longest time, reliving the horrible scene in the woods. When she finally fell asleep, the scene appeared again, only in a nightmare much worse than the reality had been. Afterwards she hadn't been able to go back to sleep, so when her mom got up, she trudged down to the kitchen in order to get some comfort and sympathy.

"Comfort and sympathy, my foot," mumbled Heather glumly.

"What did you say?" Angelica turned to her, looking puzzled.

"Oh nothing; it's just my mom. She's so preoccupied with the problems at her work that she probably wouldn't have noticed if I'd come to breakfast with two heads."

Heather shook her head. "Her boss has disappeared, right under the very nose of the investigators. They went to his home to arrest him yesterday, but the bird had flown the coop. And a pile of money had evidently flown with him. Mom was just going in to the office to answer some messages today. All of the employees have been laid off until the police figure out what's what. And when they do, it'll probably be the end of it

30

all, at least if it's true that the crook has taken off with the company's money."

"How awful!" said Angelica distractedly, glancing out the window. "Is that a car? Nope, false alarm again."

Heather rolled her eyes and went into Caliban's stall. There was no use talking to her mom, and no use talking to Angelica. The first one only thinks about her job, and the other one is on the tip of her toes just because she's borrowing a horse. Heather made a sullen grimace. She knew she was being unfair, but she couldn't help it. Right now she needed to get some help and support from somebody, but evidently the only one who had time for her was Caliban. Well, time for her might be stretching it a little far. He had his head buried in a pile of hay, so focused on eating that you'd think someone was about to snatch it away from him. Heather ruffled his mane, and then went outside to wash the saddle pad that she had put away the day before. At the time she couldn't bear the thought of starting to clean it. As she entered the saddle room, she saw a folded up piece of paper stuck underneath Caliban's saddle. A note? Quickly she took the paper and unfolded it. The note was short, but the words made her gasp.

"Forget what you saw in the woods!" it said, written in uneven, uppercase letters. Heather got furious. There was no excuse for foolish jokes like that. She had had it with stupid jokes from her friends at the stable. With the note in her hand she marched through the stable, confronting everyone she met. But nobody would admit to having written it. They just looked at her without comprehension. The last one she met was Justin. At first she thought she didn't dare, but she pulled herself together and showed him the note. Justin too denied having written it.

"But are you sure it's just a joke?" he asked with a serious expression.

"What do you mean?" Heather looked at him, uncertain. "Of course it's a joke. A very bad joke!"

31

"Maybe you're right. But regardless, it's good advice. If you're smart, you'll follow it."

Heather just stood there, staring at him with her mouth open, as he walked to the door and left.

"Isn't she fantastic? Isn't she just totally unbelievably beautiful, wonderful and magnificent?" Angelica was one big ear-to-ear smile, sitting on top of Crissy and walking her around the ring. She didn't wait for any answer from Heather, but just continued her monologue of praise.

Heather laughed and shook her head while she watched the light gray, and very elegant, filly. Apparently she had a lot of pent up energy after the transport, because Angelica had her hands full trying to make her walk forward in a somewhat collected fashion. The horse would rather have liked to jump the fence and gallop away across the fields, it looked like. Angelica would probably have liked that too, but Betty told her to stay put inside the school area on the first day, until Crissy had settled down.

Heather was glad about that. She didn't have any desire to go back to the woods, so they could just stick to riding in the ring and the school fields forever, as far as she was concerned. While she watched Angelica and Crissy, she thought about what Justin had said. Could it be that the note was not meant as a joke at all? If so, it must be the man in the woods who had been in the stable and left the note in order to threaten her. That would mean that he knew who she was and where she usually spent her time. But how was that possible?

No, it's too far fetched. Heather decided to forget about it. Why should the man bother to threaten her, when the police had disregarded her story as imagination and fabrication? She couldn't even remember what he looked like!

"But he wouldn't know that!" said Angelica, when Heather told her what she was thinking a little later.

The girls were lying on the grass by the paddock, watching Crissy and Caliban who were circling around each other guardedly. Would they make friends, or were they going to start fighting? Often, horses will bully a dapple and refuse to be near it. It's an old instinct from the time when all horses were wild and kept together in herds. Then it was important to blend into the landscape as much as possible, and an almost white horse would stick out like a sore thumb in the scenery. Such horses were therefore chased away from the herd and had to manage on their own. Heather shuddered. She could only imagine how those horses would make an easy prey for predators hunting for food.

Caliban stuck his muzzle into Crissy's mane and gave a snort. Crissy responded by neighing and giving Caliban a push. A moment later they were running side-by-side in the paddock. Heather gave a sigh of relief. The two horses had clearly accepted each other.

She turned her attention to Angelica again. "What do you mean?" she asked. "What would he not know?"

"That you don't remember what he looks like, of course! How would he know that?"

"No, of course not. He wouldn't know." Heather hadn't thought about that.

"But do you really think he..."

Angelica shook her head. "I can't imagine he would be stupid enough to sneak in here to leave a warning note for you. What good would that do? All he needs to do is lie low and stay out of sight. It would be a different matter if the police had actually found the body and were looking for the killer. Then he might have been scared that you would be able to identify him. But the way things are, he has nothing to worry about."

Heather felt almost joyful with relief. Angelica was right, of course. The note must have been meant as a joke, and she had

33

let her imagination get the best of her, largely because of what Justin had said.

"No wonder you're a little on edge after that scary incident in the woods," commented Angelica. "I've thought about it..."

"You have?" Heather looked at her, unbelieving. "I thought the only thing on your mind was a big, four-legged animal by the name of Crissy!"

Angelica laughed. "All right, all right, I know I've been going on about Crissy a lot, but can you blame me? Besides, you were just as bad when you waited for Caliban to be delivered. Have you forgotten? But be that as it may, let's talk about the mystery."

Heather looked at her with anticipation.

"I've been wondering what really happened out there in the woods after you fled on Caliban."

"The man probably got in his car and took off, don't you think? That's what I would have done if I'd been caught red-handed while burying a body!"

Angelica shook her head. "If it was that simple, the police would have found the body, right?" Heather nodded.

"So where did it go?" Angelica looked at her friend.

Heather had speculated a lot about that exact question. "I think it's most logical that he took it with him again and buried it somewhere else," she said. "And he was smart enough to leave a bag of empty bottles and that sweat suit. That was most likely just some junk lying in his car. He must have understood that I would go to the police, and that it was important to leave something there, something that resembled what I had seen."

"That was ingenious," nodded Angelica, impressed against her will. "The police bought it instantly and believed that your imagination had mistaken an innocent bag of trash for a mysterious wrapped up body."

Heather shuddered. She would never forget the horrific moment when she realized what was lying on the ground next

34

to the car. How could the police believe that she would mistake a regular trash bag filled with junk for a human? She shrugged off the frightening thought as she looked at Angelica.

"It doesn't help much that you believe what I told them I saw," she said. "The police won't lift a finger as long as they think that the dead body is just a figment of my imagination."

"I have an idea," said Angelica. "If the police won't do their job, then we'll have to do it for them!"

"What do you mean?" Heather looked at her curiously.

"Tomorrow we'll ride to the place where you saw the man dig, and then we'll start looking for tracks!"

Heather was about to object, but suddenly she felt like someone was staring at her. Don't be silly, she told herself, but the feeling was so strong that she couldn't help turning her head to check.

Justin was standing by a tree nearby. He looked at Heather with an expression that she couldn't interpret. Had he heard what they were talking about?

Chapter 6

"Here it is." Heather pointed at the bushes that still showed signs of somebody having trampled through them. "There, in the clearing, was the car, and over there, right behind the bushes, is where he was digging."

For a moment Heather envisioned the scene again, which made a chill creep up her spine. Quickly she glanced around. She didn't like being here one bit. Why had she let Angelica talk her into this?

At first Heather had blankly refused to come with Angelica to the woods, but Angelica had argued so convincingly that Heather had given in eventually.

"What could possibly be dangerous about it? You don't really believe that the murderer has taken up residence under a bush out there, do you? Surely you must understand that he's long gone by now. He's probably sitting at home congratulating himself for having fooled the police so successfully."

Heather had to reluctantly admit that Angelica had a point, and before she knew it she had promised to go along. She regretted it now, but it was too late.

Normally Heather thoroughly enjoyed riding Caliban, but this morning she barely even noticed sitting on his back, that's how tense she was. Fortunately Caliban hadn't noticed anything unusual. He was walking calmly into the woods, side by side with Crissy, apparently happy to go for a ride with his new best friend.

Heather sat as stiff as a statue on Caliban's back while Angelica jumped down on the ground.

Angelica looked up at Heather. "Are you getting down, or what?" she asked.

Heather shook her head. Not on her life was she getting off the horse. She knew it was ridiculous, but she expected to see a man jumping out of the bushes any moment now, and if she were on the ground she'd be a sitting duck for him.

"I don't care if you think I'm a stupid coward," she said, "but this place gives me the creeps. Can't we just forget the whole thing and go back? What are you expecting to find, anyway?"

Angelica handed her Crissy's reins and stepped through the bushes. "I have no idea," she said. "Some clue, or a track of the man or the car, I guess. I honestly don't know."

"But if he took the body with him, then there's no use in looking here, is there? He could have buried it on the opposite side of town, as far as we know."

"I doubt that very much," said Angelica from the other side of the bushes. "If you were standing here with a dead body, knowing that the police were coming, would you risk driving around with it, clear across town? What if the police had put up road barriers and stopped all cars coming from this part of town?"

"I don't know what I would have done, because fortunately I've never killed anybody," said Heather. "But maybe you're right."

She thought about it for a moment, and then said, "If I had to hide the body in a different place, and I expected the police to show up at any moment, I would definitely not have started digging another hole somewhere. It must have taken him quite a bit of time to dig that hole where the police found the trash bag."

Angelica straightened up as she looked at Heather. "You're absolutely right! He had to figure out something else to do with it!"

"The Linden Pond!" Heather burst out. "In detective movies they always dump the body in the water, and then some poor fisherman catches it on his hook because the murderer used some no-good weight which came loose, making the body float to the top. Ugh! The thought of it makes me sick. Can we go home now? I don't think this is exciting at all; just disgusting."

"Do what you want, but I'm going to the pond to look for tracks."

Angelica swung herself into Crissy's saddle, kicked her into motion and directed her onto the trail.

Heather just sat there looking at her leaving, while she, with great effort, tried to hold Caliban back from following them. He didn't understand why he couldn't go with Crissy. Heather patted him on the neck and talked to him in a calming way. Just as Angelica disappeared out of sight between the trees, Heather suddenly realized that if she were going to go home now, she would have to ride all alone through the woods. Suddenly she felt as if the trees were moving closer together and someone was watching her, wanting to stop her from getting home. She knew perfectly well that it was sheer nonsense, but she wasn't able to shrug off her fears. To ride home alone suddenly seemed much scarier than helping Angelica look for tracks.

Quickly Heather kicked Caliban into motion. He practically danced along the trail, eager to catch up to Crissy. "Wait for me!" she called out to Angelica. "I changed my mind. I'm coming!"

"This is no use! Let's give up." Heather held Caliban still, looking at Angelica. The two girls had ridden back and forth along the Linden Pond for more than an hour, searching every millimeter of the grounds. At least that's how it felt. Heather's eyes were sore from staring for so long, and they hadn't seen anything suspicious.

Angelica shook her head stubbornly. "Just five more minutes," she said. "There is one more trail he could have used if he drove down to the water. It ends over there." She pointed.

"If there's nothing there either, we'll give up. I promise. Okay?"

"Fine," said Heather grudgingly. To tell the truth, she was really glad they had not found anything. The thought of a person lying at the bottom of the pond terrified her. Clearly Angelica saw this as an exciting adventure, but she hadn't experienced what Heather had.

Heather's thoughts wandered to Justin as she followed behind Angelica and Crissy. He had been so sweet and considerate toward her when she came into the stable this morning. Heather had felt exhausted and depressed after another night of nightmares, having relived the scene in the woods again.

Justin had asked if she was okay, because she seemed so tired and out of it. Heather told him about the nightmare. This time the faceless man had grabbed her arm and raised the shovel as if about to hit her. Just as he swung, she had woken up, scared to death and soaked in sweat.

Justin didn't comment on her dream. He had just stroked her briefly on the arm and said it was smart of her to stay away from the woods, as she had done the day before. Then her nightmare would probably go away soon.

Heather felt all warm and fuzzy inside from the touch of his hand. Should she ask him if he wanted to go for a ride with her and Angelica, today maybe? Did she have the guts? What if he said no... what if...

Before Heather had had a chance to make up her mind, Angelica had come running in, full of plans for their big search in the woods. When Heather went looking for Justin a little later, she saw to her disappointment that he and Bogart had taken off already.

"Hey! Come and look at this!" Angelica's voice pulled Heather back to the present moment.

"What is it?"

"Car tracks." Angelica pointed.

39

The tracks led down a gentle slope all the way to the edge of the water. About halfway the tracks were deeper, as if the car had gotten stuck in the mud and the wheels had been spinning.

Heather felt her heart start beating faster. Was it possible...?

She threw a quick, anxious glance toward the water, as if she half expected to see the plastic bag with the body floating to the surface. But the smooth and untouched surface of the water didn't reveal anything about what might be hidden down on the bottom.

Angelica and Heather looked at each other. "Now what do we do?" asked Heather.

"Call the police," said Angelica with a firm voice.

Heather felt a sudden jolt in her stomach. What did Angelica say yesterday? That Heather was safe as long as the murderer felt safe. But if they called the police now, and the body actually was lying somewhere in the water, what would the murderer do then? Would he go into hiding, hoping the case would never be solved? Or would he try to get rid of the only person who had seen him and knew what he looked like? At least he thought she did....

Heather felt a chill creep up her spine. She wished more than anything that she could just gallop home and forget about everything that had happened. But she knew what she had to do. Reluctantly, she pulled out her cell phone. But what was the number for the police station? She looked at Angelica, at a loss.

"I guess we could call 911," said Angelica after having thought about it. "This isn't exactly an emergency, but maybe they can transfer you to somebody else at the police. Do you remember the names of the two police officers that you spoke to last time?"

Heather thought really hard. "One of them was Kiss... Kess... yes, Kessinger I think it was."

Hesitatingly, she started dialing the number. Then she stopped. "No, I don't dare to do it," she said. "Can't we just ride back to the stable and ask Betty to call instead? She's a grown up, so they're more likely to listen to her than to us."

Angelica shook her head. "We call now," she said. "I'll do it if you won't."

She bent down and snatched the phone out of Heather's hand, then dialed 911. When someone answered, Angelica asked for Officer Kessinger. There was a long silence.

"Please answer," mumbled Angelica, as if she could nudge the officer to pick up the phone.

"Maybe he's not in," suggested Heather.

"Yes, they said he was in... wait, something's happening now. Hello? Is this Officer Kessinger?"

Apparently this was confirmed, because Angelica started explaining who she was and who Heather was, and what they had discovered.

"Excuse me? Give me a break!" Angelica frowned and looked angry. "Are you suggesting that I'm just sitting around calling the police for fun? I demand that you take me seriously. I know you said last time that nobody was reported missing, but that doesn't mean..."

Angelica was interrupted. "What? You've got what, you say?" She listened silently for a while, and then said numbly, "Okay. Thank you, Officer."

Heather looked at her, dismally. "I knew it," she said. "They didn't believe you and they're not going to do anything."

"Wrong on both accounts," said Angelica with a triumphant smile. "Officer Kessinger was totally disinterested at first, and just wanted to get rid of me. But then something happened. While he was talking to me, he evidently got a message about a man who has been reported missing. And they suspect that 'something of a criminal nature might have happened to him,' as Kessinger so eloquently put it. What an idiotic, roundabout way of saying things! But never mind that, at least he said he will take a look at the tracks, and told us to wait here until they arrive."

It seemed like an eternity before the policemen finally showed up on the trail. Angelica waved them toward her, and showed them the wheel tracks. They thanked her politely, and told the girls to go home. They would contact them later if it became necessary, said one of the policemen.

"Clearly, he thought that they might find something," said Heather as she and Angelica rode back through the woods.

Angelica shrugged her shoulders. "Maybe they will, maybe they won't. At least we've done what we can, and now we deserve a gallop. Race you to the end of the trail! Ready, set, go!"

The horses rushed forward, side by side. The riders yelled loudly in excitement. Neither of them noticed a figure standing motionless between the trees. The person peered at them with narrow eyes and an irritated expression. Darned girls snooping around in places they should have stayed far away from. This could get dangerous. Something had to be done, and quickly...

Chapter 7

"Have you heard?" Heather was just putting away her bicycle outside the stable as Angelica came running toward her.

"Heard what?"

"It was on the news this morning! The police have searched the Linden pond and found a dead man. He was wrapped in gray plastic just like you said. I bet those police officers aren't quite so haughty anymore. I hope they remember to thank us for solving the case for them."

Heather gaped at her. "Are you serious?" she eventually said. "I haven't heard the news today. Mom had a phone call just as we were about to eat breakfast. She had to leave right away. I have no idea what was so important, but she rushed out of the house as if it was a matter of life and death."

"Maybe the police have arrested her boss and found the money he took," suggested Angelica absentmindedly. "But never mind that right now. Just think, we were right about the body! Are we geniuses or what? How about we just drop school and start a detective service."

"Sure!" Heather laughed. "By the way, it's all thanks to you, not me. I didn't want to go looking for tracks at all."

"Do you think the police have caught the murderer already?" said Heather over her shoulder as she walked through the stable door. "I hope... ooops!" she said as she walked right into a person who was on his way out. Justin!

Heather felt her cheeks get warm. "H... hi," she stammered in a fluster.

Justin mumbled something she didn't catch and disappeared

out the door. Heather looked at the door closing behind him, perplexed. What was the matter with him? Was he mad at her for some reason?

The next moment she totally forgot about Justin. As she came into Caliban's stall, she saw a white piece of paper pinned to the wall with a big yellow thumbtack. The paper was folded up twice. Heather's first reaction was anger. Who was stupid enough to hang a note inside the stall like this? What if Caliban had loosened the note and swallowed the thumbtack?

She took down the paper and put the thumbtack carefully in her pocket. Caliban pushed her arm with his muzzle, wanting some attention. She scratched his forehead distractedly while she unfolded the note. He snorted contentedly as he slobbered on her arm. Heather barely even noticed. She stared at the note like she was hypnotized. *Think about your horse! Continue to forget me!*

Heather felt a wave of nausea. This was no joke, that's for sure. Her legs suddenly felt like jelly and she sank down on the straw-covered floor, still with her eyes glued to the note. Caliban nudged her playfully with his muzzle. *What are you doing*, he seemed to say. *Where's my food?*

Heather didn't pay any attention to him. Thoughts were jumping around in her mind like boisterous foals. Who could have been in the stable? The murderer? Who else could it be? If so, he knew that she couldn't remember him; that was clear from the note. But how was that possible? Was he keeping an eye on her? Had he been spying on her ever since that horrible day in the woods? Maybe he had walked right past her and gloated about the fact that she didn't recognize him. Was he nearby right now? Outside? Or maybe inside the stable?

Heather jumped up so fast she lost her balance and crashed into the wall with a bang. Caliban jerked back in shock, shaking his head. Heather looked around in panic. Eva and Megan, two younger girls who were getting their horses ready for a riding lesson, were looking at her with surprise. Just the other day Heather had scolded them for running and being noisy in the stable, and here she was, making all kinds of commotion herself. What was the matter with her?

"Sorry, I lost my balance," said Heather, trying not to let on that anything was wrong.

Megan shrugged her shoulders and the girls continued what they were doing.

"Scary!" said Angelica after Heather had showed her the note. "I can't believe the guy would risk coming here to threaten you. What are you going to do? Tell Betty?"

Heather shook her head. "I intend to do exactly what he's telling me to do," she said. "Can't you see he's threatening to hurt Caliban? I won't risk anything happening to him. Besides, I've already told the police everything I know."

"Then you've got nothing to worry about."

Heather looked up with a start. Justin was standing outside Crissy's stall, looking at her. "Sorry if I scared you," he said, smiling. "I thought you could hear me."

His smile made Heather's heart skip a few beats.

"No... I... we were so absorbed by what we where talking about, I probably wouldn't have noticed if a herd of elephants walked in here," stammered Heather.

Justin laughed and she knew she was blushing again. A herd of elephants...? Why would she say something so silly? Justin must think she was a total dimwit for sure.

But actually it didn't look like he did. He hung around and chatted with them for quite a while. Heather showed him the note she had found. He looked at it carefully, and then said slowly, "Of course it's none of my business, but I think you'd be smart to lie low after this. It could be very dangerous to get involved in a murder case. So my advice is, stay out of it and leave it to the police to find the guy. You don't remember any-

45

thing more about him anyway, do you?" He looked closely at her.

Heather shook her head. "I have the same nightmare every single night," she said as she shuffled straw with the tip of her boot. "But his face is always in a cloud. Maybe I'll never remember it."

"Probably just as well," said Justin reassuringly, giving her shoulder a quick hug. "That way you won't have to get involved again." He looked at his watch and burst out, "Gosh, I'd better go. I promised my mom to run some errands for her. See you later!"

With that, he was gone. Heather watched him until he was out of sight, wishing he hadn't left. The stable felt so much safer when he was around.

Heather was tired and felt as heavy as lead as she biked home later in the afternoon. She hoped her mom wasn't home. Right now she just wanted to get in the house and be alone for a while. Fortunately, the house was quiet and empty when she got there. She went to the kitchen and drank a glass of water. Then she ran up to her room, changed out of her riding clothes, and threw herself on the bed. She lay down on top of the bedspread looking at the ceiling, while her thoughts wandered back to what had happened earlier in the day.

Right after Justin had left, the police arrived, wanting to talk to Heather and Angelica. Angelica had urged Heather to tell the police about the warning note, but she had flatly refused to do so. She finally convinced Angelica, however reluctantly, to agree to keep quiet about it, at least for now. The police asked if Heather and Angelica wanted their parents present while they talked to them, but the girls declined this. That would just have caused a lot of commotion.

"Besides, my mom has been in bed with a migraine for a couple of days," said Angelica, "so I haven't even told her

46

anything about all this yet. No need to get her all worried for no reason."

"Dad is overseas on a business trip, and my mom had an important meeting today," Heather chimed in. "She flew out the door so fast, I think it must have been something very important."

The police officers looked at each other. Then one of them cleared his throat as he said, "Your mother works at Gold Enterprises, doesn't she?"

Heather nodded her head in surprise. How did he know that?

The policeman glanced over at his colleague and cleared his throat again. "You might as well know," he said. "It'll be on the news tonight anyway. The dead man that you helped us find has been identified. His name was John Simmons."

"Mom's boss?" said Heather, shocked. She stared at the policeman with a disbelieving expression on her face.

"But he... he ran away. At least that's what my mom said... that he'd apparently taken off with a bunch of money that belonged to the company."

The police officer nodded. "That's what we all believed at first," he said. "Everything seemed like a clear-cut case. But then we got some information that showed that the reality of it was somewhat different. Mr. Simmons got involved in a lot of illegal activities while running Gold Enterprises. I'll spare you the details, but it's all about smuggling, bribery, and money laundering involving large sums of money. When Mr. Simmons realized that things were starting to heat up around him, his first intention was to run. But it's not as simple as it may seem to get a fake ID and live in hiding from the police. Therefore he decided on a simpler solution for himself. He was willing to tell the police everything they needed to know to bust the whole gangster ring in return for a lesser charge against himself."

"I see," said Angelica excitedly. "And when the others found out what he was planning to do, they killed him."

"That's probably correct, more or less. Mr. Simmons was killed by a blow to the temple; hence we can't be sure if the murder was planned or if it happened during an argument. Either way, the killer had to get rid of the body and chose the most isolated area he could find at the moment. Little did he know that he would be seen by a curious horseback rider just as he was about to get rid of his victim."

"But you do have a suspect, right?" asked Heather hopefully. She wished with all her heart that the policeman would say that it was only a matter of time, or preferably minutes, until they had the culprit in custody.

But the police officers quickly crushed her wishful thinking. They told her that the bottles and the sweat suit, which had been buried instead of the body, had been examined and checked for fingerprints.

"We found a lot of prints," one of the policemen said, "but we don't know who they belong to yet. None of them matched any of the prints that are already in the police records, so as far as that goes, we're nowhere. The prints won't be useful until we arrest a suspect and are able to compare."

Heather rode into the woods. It was beautiful weather and she was singing out loud. The birds all around her were chirping happily. She bent down and patted Caliban's neck, and he responded by increasing his tempo. A cute little rabbit jumped in front of them on the trail, then disappeared into the bushes. Poor little thing, it had probably gotten lost. Heather wondered if she should ride after it and try to catch the rabbit, but decided not to as she realized she didn't have much time. It had started getting dark. Then she saw a car. What was it doing here in the middle of the forest? The car meant danger; she could feel it. She pulled on Caliban's reins trying to turn him around, but he continued on as if nothing had happened. Then she heard the sound of a shovel hitting the ground, again and again.

48

Suddenly she was overwhelmed with fear, but there was nothing she could do to stop Caliban. They reached the bushes. The man who was digging had not heard her yet. On the ground next to him was a bundle, wrapped in plastic. All of a sudden the man looked up and saw her.

"So you're here again," he said. His face was shrouded in fog, but she could tell by his voice that he was smiling. "Come closer; I've got plenty of room for both you and your horse."

"Don't you dare touch my horse!" screamed Heather.

The man laughed, a creepy, rumbling laughter. Then he stretched out his arms.

Fortunately I'm too far away for him to catch me, thought Heather. But then his arms started growing. They got longer and longer and came closer and closer toward her. Suddenly his hands transformed into horrifying claws which tried to grab Caliban.

Heather woke up screaming, and looked around in panic. Where was she? She felt an enormous relief as she realized that she was in her own, safe bed. The dream had been different this time. Before the man had been after her, now it was Caliban who was in danger.

The dream must have changed because of that creepy note, thought Heather as she lay down again, trying to go back to sleep.

As she did, she heard a sound. Was someone walking downstairs? At this time, in the middle of the night? Heather listened intently. Was it her mom rummaging around downstairs? But in the same instant she heard a couple of loud snores from the room next to hers. That was a familiar sound. Her mom was in her bed, sleeping, no doubt about that. Next she heard a squeaking sound and something scraping. She couldn't tell if the sound came from inside or outside the house. Her heart was beating hard now. There was a click, and afterward everything got quiet. Heather was listening so hard her ears must be stretching. But she didn't hear any more suspicious sounds. Did she dare go downstairs and check, or should she wake her mom?

She got out of bed and tiptoed over to the window. She saw nothing unusual, so she proceeded to the door. But here her courage failed her. She simply couldn't bring herself to go out in the hall. If there were burglars downstairs, let them just take whatever they wanted! Before going back to bed, Heather grabbed a chair and leaned it against the door under the doorknob. She felt a little stupid as she slinked back into bed, crawling under the covers again. She lay there alert and listening for a long time, but everything was silent. Even so she felt that somebody had been in the house, somebody who didn't belong there.

Chapter 8

Heather woke up to the sound of the door pushing against the chair. Somebody was trying to get in! She sat up, dizzy and sleepy, peering toward the doorknob which was moving.

"Who is it?" she asked, uneasy.

"It's me," said her mom's voice from the other side. "Can I come in? Why have you locked the door?"

Heather slipped out of bed, removed the chair and jumped back under the covers again.

"It's open now!" she shouted.

Her mom opened the door and came into the room. "Sorry if I woke you," she said with a smile to Heather. Fortunately she didn't say anything more about the locked door.

"I just wanted to let you know that I'm going to the office now. The police said they would come and talk to all of us, to find out if we know anything that might shed some light on the murder of Mr. Simmons."

Heather nodded. "You said that last night," she mumbled, still not completely awake. "What time is it anyway?"

"Eight thirty."

Heather sat up. What? Good grief! She should have been at the stable quite a while ago.

"Take it easy," said her mom. "I called Betty and she promised to give Caliban his breakfast. The rest can wait until later. I thought you might need to sleep after the strain you've been under lately."

She sat down by Heather on the edge of the bed. "There's something I have to talk to you about before I go," she said

51

seriously. "I didn't want to say anything last night because I don't want to scare you. But there's no way around it. As long as the murderer is out there, you're not really safe, and you need to keep that in mind. You saw a murderer, and you're the only one who can identify the man if you should happen to remember what he looks like."

Her mom looked urgently at her. "I want you to promise me that you won't go anywhere alone, and that you will stay close to the riding school. No more rides out to the woods until the murderer has been caught. It's possible that I'm being overly nervous and that the guy has gone into hiding somewhere and doesn't have a clue who you are, but I don't want you to take any chances. After all, he saw you riding a horse, so if he starts keeping an eye on the riding schools nearby..."

Her mother was silent for a moment. "I'm going to talk to the police about this," she said, "and ask them what they will do to protect you. But in the meantime you must promise me to be careful!"

"I promise."

Her mom got up and got ready to leave. Heather felt a pang of fear in her chest. She had been perfectly aware of the danger already, but now that her mom had talked about it too, it became even more real and frightening. And her mom still didn't know about the threatening note that Heather had received. For a moment Heather was tempted to call for her mom to come back and tell her about it, but she changed her mind. If her mom found out that the murderer already knew who she was, she'd probably lock her up or force her to come with her to the office, to sit there all day. And if they didn't catch the murderer for a long time, it could be an eternity before Heather got to go to the stable or do anything at all on her own.

There was still a possibility that the note was just a bad joke, and if so she would have frightened her mother for no reason. Heather decided to not say anything, at least not yet.

She got up, threw on her clothes, and had a quick breakfast. She'd never noticed before how empty and ominous the house seemed when no one else was around. There were creaks and squeaks everywhere, and she kept thinking she heard somebody walking in the hallway. When she eventually got up the courage to go out and check, she saw that the front door was locked, so obviously it was just her imagination.

Heather put on her shoes, grabbed her cell phone, and went out to the shed to get her bike. To her surprise she noticed that the door to the shed was not locked. That's strange. She was sure she had locked it after she put away her bike last night. Could it be that her mom had been out here and had forgotten to lock it? That didn't seem very likely. Her mom was extremely careful about such things. Had there been burglars here? She opened the door somewhat hesitatingly and peeked inside. No sign of any burglary. Her bike was exactly where she had left it, and her parents' bikes were also where they belonged. Feeling relieved, she entered the shed. Then she noticed something white sticking out under her bike seat. With shaky hands, she pulled out the paper and unfolded it. Then she had to sit down because her legs would not carry her any longer. She sat on the floor for quite a while just staring at the note, feeling an icy chill creep up her spine, and her head started tingling with fear. The sounds she had heard last night had not been her imagination after all. He had been here, at her home, and he had left another threatening note. The words were written in the same uneven uppercase letters as last time. There was no mistaking the message.

Do you understand now how easy it is? it said. *If you know what's good for you, you'll forget me!*

What was she going to do? She was unable to think clearly. The letters on the paper danced in front of her eyes and became a blurred jumble. Heather got up on unsteady legs and looked around. Her fear had taken hold of her chest like a claw. Quickly she stuffed the note in her pocket, grabbed her bike and went outside. As fast as she could, she biked to the stable, all the while casting fearful glances around. Where was he? In a car? Behind a bush? He could be anywhere, and she was safe only as long as it suited him.

"What's the rush?" said Betty with a smile, as Heather pedaled into the stable yard.

Heather was so out of breath she couldn't answer.

"Did you think Caliban went hungry while you slept?" Betty shook her head. "I told your mom I would feed him."

Heather nodded and put her bike away. "I know, it's... it's..."

"Take it easy," said Betty, who misinterpreted her facial expression. "You don't have to feel bad about coming late for once. Some other time it'll be me needing a favor." She smiled and went into her office.

Heather hurried into the stable. Angelica was standing in Crissy's stall, and waved when she saw her. "Good heavens, you're all hot and sweaty!" she said as Heather came closer. "You look like you just ran a marathon or something."

"Only biking for my life," said Heather quietly.

Angelica looked at her quizzically. "Did something happen?" she asked.

Heather thought for a second. Should she tell Angelica? Yes, she simply had to talk to someone, or she would go crazy.

"Come over to Caliban's stall when you're done with Crissy," she said.

"I am done," said Angelica, following her. "C'mon, tell me. You've got me curious."

Heather went over to Caliban and dug her fingers into his mane. Caliban responded by rubbing his head against her arm. The warmth of his big body felt comforting. Heather knew she would do anything to protect him. She would not let that evil man do anything to hurt him.

"But what if your memory comes back and you remember

54

what he looks like?" asked Angelica after Heather had told her what had happened. "Aren't you going to tell them anything then?"

Heather shook her head. "I can't," she said finally, looking at the floor. "I'm so afraid of what he might do to Caliban. He proved last night that he can get in wherever he wants to, whenever he wants to. So if I tell them anything, he'll have no problem breaking into the stable to hurt Caliban."

Or kill him! was the next thought that shot through her head, a thought so horrible she couldn't say it out loud.

Angelica looked at her in disbelief. "Are you out of your mind?" she said. "The guy is a murderer! Of course you must help them catch him if you can! If you help the police to find him and arrest him, he can't hurt you, don't you understand that?"

"That's easy enough for you to say," hissed Heather. Her despair over Angelica not understanding was almost more than she could bear right now. "It's not you or your horse he's threatening. How would you feel if it was Crissy who was the target?"

"I would still do my duty! Nobody can threaten me into silence," said Angelica with a stubborn expression, pointing her nose in the air.

Heather couldn't take anymore. She broke into tears. "This is all your fault," she gasped. "If you hadn't forced me to go along to look for tracks, the body wouldn't have been found and I would've been safe. And Caliban too."

"What a load of horse manure!" gushed Angelica angrily. "You would never have been able to forget what you saw, and you would have spent the rest of your life speculating what really happened to the body. You should be glad that the case is almost solved, and that you can put it behind you."

"But the case is not solved, don't you see that?" Heather looked up at Angelica with red, teary eyes. "The murderer is still out there and he's threatening me! I don't dare say anything!" Her voice rose to a shrill.

"Hey, what's going on here? Has something happened?"

Justin had entered the stable. He came over to Caliban's stall and looked at Heather with a worried expression. In the middle of her despair Heather still couldn't help feeling perturbed at the fact that Justin got to see her like this, with red puffy eyes and her nose all shiny from crying. She bent her head in an attempt to hide behind her hair, while hissing at Angelica. "Don't you dare tell a soul about this!"

"Relax," said Angelica. "I'll be as silent as a grave. But I think you're behaving like a total idiot, just so you know."

She tossed her head as she left the stall. Justin came in and squatted down next to Heather. Neither of them said anything for a while. Then Justin reached his arm out and stroked her hair gently.

"I can see that something has scared you," he said quietly.

"I don't want to talk about it," mumbled Heather. She regretted bitterly having told Angelica.

"That's all right, I won't push you," said Justin softly. "But you shouldn't sit in here and be depressed all day. How about going for a ride?"

Heather's heart skipped a beat. "That sounds nice," she said hesitatingly. She remembered her mom's warning and added, "But I don't want to ride in the woods, I've had enough of that place for a while!"

"That's understandable," said Justin as he got up. "We could ride across the fields over to the lake. Maybe we could go for a swim with the horses."

"I don't have a swim suit with me," said Heather as she got up too. "But I guess we could go wading with the horses at least."

"Super idea! I'll come too," said Angelica, who just walked past them.

56

Heather felt a pang of disappointment. She had hoped that Justin and she could go for a ride, just the two of them. But she couldn't very well say that to Angelica.

"Look at Crissy, she's scared of the water!" Angelica laughed as she tried to steer her horse into the shallow water. But Crissy wouldn't budge. She thrashed her head and gave an ear-splitting neigh. *Wade? What's this nonsense?* she seemed to say. *Nobody is going to get me into that yucky wet stuff, thank you very much!*

"Look at Caliban and Bogart; they're in the water," pleaded Angelica in her most soothing voice. Crissy merely snorted. She couldn't care less what kind of dumb things the other horses were willing to do. As for her, she intended to stay on dry ground where it was safe, and that was that! Angelica finally gave up. She tethered Crissy to a tree, looking at Heather and Justin who were laughing and splashing water at each other.

"I'm glad I came," said Heather on the top of her breath a little later as they rode back onto dry land to take a break.

"I'm glad you came too," said Justin, looking her straight in the eyes.

Heather felt a warmth spread all the way to her toes. *He likes me!* she thought with a thrill.

A little later Heather was stretched out in the grass, only halfway listening to Angelica who was telling a somewhat drawn out joke which she had heard before. For the first time in what seemed like a long time, she could feel herself relax. All the scary things that had happened seemed far away and totally unreal, more like a bad dream. Heather noticed that she was sleepy. No wonder, because she hadn't gotten much sleep the last few nights.

She blocked out the sound of Angelica's voice as she watched some light clouds sailing across the sky. One of them looked like a hippopotamus with his mouth wide open. Then it looked like it was transforming into a cow... no, a horse. The horse was brown and looked exactly like Caliban. Sure, it was he. But how did they get here, way into the woods? She was sitting on the horse's back looking around. Ahead of her was the riding trail, extending into the thicket of trees. Then she heard the sound of a shovel digging into the ground. Curious, she rode closer and caught sight of a man. He straightened up and looked at her. "I knew you'd remember me eventually," he said as he looked straight at her. This time his face was not hidden in a fog. She saw him quite clearly. His eyes flashed an evil look as he raised the shovel and threw it at Heather, who screamed and threw herself aside. She hit something soft and warm. It had arms, which grabbed her and held her back. Heather thrashed and struggled in a panic to free herself.

"Heather!" said a voice. "Wake up! It's just a dream!"

Heather opened her eyes, all confused as she saw Justin's face in front of her. A feeling of relief washed over her; it had only been a dream. Then it hit her, the man's face, she had seen it completely clearly! And she could still remember it quite clearly. Now she knew what the murderer looked like! She opened her mouth to say so, but closed it again. She'd better think this through.

She was still thinking really hard as she was riding back a little later. If she told Angelica that she remembered the murderer's face, she knew what Angelica would say. She would pressure Heather to go to the police with her description of the man. But Heather didn't feel ready to do that yet. Should she confide in Justin instead? No, that would make Angelica get all offended. Besides, she didn't know Justin that well. It would probably be better to keep quiet until she had decided what she wanted to do about it.

She bent down and patted Caliban on the neck. She mustn't do anything that could put him in danger.

58

But if you don't tell, then how will you ever be able to feel safe? said a little voice inside her. *What if you suddenly run into the murderer by chance at a store or in the street? You wouldn't be able to hide your fear.*

"Oh, shut up!" said Heather irritably to the voice inside.

"Who? Me?" Justin looked at her, surprised.

Heather blushed. She hadn't meant to say it out loud. "No, I'm sorry. I was just yelling at myself," she said, feeling pretty stupid. "Because I can't make up my mind."

Justin looked at her quizzically, but when she didn't say anything more, he started talking about something else.

Chapter 9

Later that afternoon, while Heather was grooming and feeding Caliban, she was still contemplating whether or not she should tell someone about the dream and what it had revealed. Caliban could tell that she was distracted. She'd usually chat with him and pat and scratch him in between the grooming, but today she hadn't said a word for quite a while. Caliban wasn't used to being ignored like that. He started stomping his feet and nipping at her sweater in order to get some attention. She didn't notice until he pressed his muzzle into her hair, slobbering yellowish-green hay down her neck.

"Yuck! That's disgusting!" she laughed, pushing his muzzle away. Caliban looked at her with his big, dark eyes. Heather thought she saw a look of reproach.

She scratched his forehead and stroked him across the bridge of his nose.

"I'm sorry, sweetie," she said. "I didn't mean to ignore you. I've just got so much to think about, you see."

But Caliban didn't care one bit about that. How could anything possibly be more important than him? But, since he had her attention again, he seemed to forgive her. He blew his warm breath once more into her neck, before lowering his head and going back to eating his hay. Second only to attention, food was the most important thing in his world, no doubt about that.

"You're lucky, not having a worry in the world," said Heather as she watched him enviously.

"Maybe you would be less worried if you'd tell me what's bothering you."

Heather gave a sudden start. She hadn't heard Angelica approaching.

"You were as quiet as a mouse and totally distant the whole way home," said Angelica. "Was it that nightmare you had that scared you so much?"

Heather nodded and made a sudden decision. "I remember him!" she said quietly.

At first Angelica just stared at her without comprehension, and then she got it. "You mean...?"

Heather nodded. "I was back in the woods, and this time I saw his face just as clearly as I see yours right now."

"You have to tell the police." Angelica spoke with a firm voice.

Heather shook her head. "I don't know," she said helplessly. "What if he takes revenge on Caliban?"

"You will have to take that risk. Besides, the police can probably keep the stable under surveillance until the guy is arrested."

Heather looked doubtfully at her. "Do you really think they're going to bother looking after a horse?"

"Who wouldn't bother looking after horses?" asked Justin curiously. He had finished grooming and feeding Bogart and was coming over to the girls.

"Oh, it's just Angelica who thinks that Caliban needs police protection," said Heather, laughing it off as a joke.

"And why would she think that? Did something happen?" Justin looked inquiringly at them both.

"No, nothing," said Angelica quickly, before Heather could say anything. "I was just saying it because of that note, you know..."

Justin nodded. "Well, as long as Heather doesn't remember anything, there's probably no danger," he said.

"How can you be so sure?" demanded Heather.

"Just pure logic," said Justin. "I know you're afraid. And that guy is definitely not to be fooled with. But if he meant to finish you off or something like that, he could easily have done it already, right? Instead he has given you several warnings – both here at the stable *and* at your home. Which shows that he doesn't really want to hurt you. He just wants to make sure you don't give him away to the police. So you should just do as he says, then nothing will happen."

Heather turned around to ask Angelica what she thought. But to her surprise, her friend wasn't standing next to them anymore. She was heading for the door.

"Where're you going?" Heather called to her.

"I just remembered that I have to ask Betty something before she takes off to start the lessons," shouted Angelica over her shoulder. "I'll be right back."

Heather felt a jolt of anguish in her stomach. Was Angelica going to tell Betty what Heather had confided in her? If she did, the police might show up at the stable before she could blink an eye.

Almost 15 minutes passed before Angelica came back. Justin had gone out to look for a friend he had agreed to meet.

Heather was pacing back and forth like a caged tiger while waiting for Angelica. As soon as her friend showed up, she confronted her. "What did you want with Betty?" she demanded to know.

"Hey, take it easy! What's the matter with you?" Angelica shook her head.

"Did you tell Betty what we talked about earlier today?" Heather looked at her with an accusatory look.

"Of course not!" Angelica looked offended. "Do you actually think I would do that without asking you first?"

"Sorry." Heather looked down. "It was just the way you disappeared, just as we were talking about the murder, and..."

"If you must know, I haven't been to see Betty at all," said Angelica. "I just had to get out for a while to think."

"Think about what?"

But Angelica wouldn't tell her what bothered her, no matter how much Heather asked and begged.

Maybe she had gone to Betty and spilled the beans after all, but didn't want to admit it, thought Heather while she biked home that evening. She couldn't see any other explanation for Angelica's strange behavior.

Just as she was about to cross the street, she looked over her shoulder to check for approaching cars. Further down the street she saw a white car approaching at a slow speed. Her heart gave a start. Hadn't she seen that same car as she turned onto the road by the stable too? Her heart started beating faster. Was it following her? No, suddenly it turned down a side street and disappeared. Heather gave a sigh of relief. She was just letting her imagination get the best of her, she thought. Even so, she didn't feel safe until she unlocked the door at home and heard her mom ask if she had had a good day.

Chapter 10

The next morning Heather biked to the stable really early. Before she went home the day before, Angelica had pleaded with her to go to the police. "Think it over until tomorrow," she said, and Heather had promised to do that. That wasn't so hard, because she wasn't able to think about much else anyway.

Deep inside, she was hoping that maybe the police would have found out who the man was by now, so that she wouldn't have to say anything. But according to her mom, the police didn't appear to have any leads in the case, and they didn't say anything on the news either that would indicate that the case was any closer to being solved.

Heather felt tired and heavy in the head. She hadn't slept much last night either, and she knew this couldn't go on much longer. Maybe she should be listening to Angelica and not to Justin. As always, the thought of Justin made her heart beat a little faster and she was glad to see his bike outside the stable. That meant that he was here already.

The stable door was cracked, and it opened without making a sound when Heather pushed on it. As she walked down the hallway, she heard someone talking. She looked around, but couldn't see anybody. Then she realized that the voice came from the saddle room. Was it Justin who was talking in there? Who was he talking to? Betty?

Heather hesitated for a moment. Yes, it was Justin's voice, no doubt about that. Just then she heard her own name mentioned. Curiosity made her walk quietly a little closer. A part of her was ashamed to be listening in on a private conversation, but at the same time she wanted desperately to know what he was saying about her.

She stopped. It was totally quiet in there now. Then she heard Justin's voice again, and it occurred to her that he must be alone in there and was talking to somebody on his cell phone.

"No," she heard him say. "How many times do I have to tell you that everything is under control? She is doing as I say, I'm sure of it. Yes, I placed it in the shed, just like you said, and no, she still doesn't remember anything, so you can just relax! Just stay away from her, do you hear?"

Heather could barely stifle a gasp. Her heartbeat thundered so loud inside her, she felt like he must hear it. She retreated as quietly as she could, over to the door and out to the stable yard. Once outside, she slipped around the corner where she stood bent over, gasping for breath. Thoughts were churning in her head and she felt like she was going to be sick.

She didn't dare to go back into the stable until she saw Justin ride out on Bogart. He was headed in the direction of the woods. Heather watched him until he was out of sight. Then she ran as fast as her trembling legs would carry her into the stable and over to Caliban's stall. He greeted her good morning with an excited neigh. Like a robot, she patted him on the neck and brought him an armful of hay. While he eagerly munched on the savory straws, Heather sank down in the corner of the stall, burying her head in her hands. That's how she still sat when Angelica arrived a little while later, entering the stable and sticking her head over the wall of the stall to say hi.

"What happened?" she asked in a shocked voice.

Heather looked up at her with a distraught look on her face. "It's Justin!" she said with a stifle. "He's in on it!"

"So I was right!" exclaimed Angelica. "I didn't want to say anything yesterday, because I wasn't sure, but..." She thought for a moment. "Hold on a second. Let me just throw some food to that greedy horse of mine," she said. "Then we'll talk."

A couple of minutes later she was back. "C'mon," she said. "Let's sit outside in the sunshine and watch the lessons while we talk. That way people can't sneak up on us and listen to what we're saying."

Heather followed her like an obedient dog. She felt as if she was walking beside herself after the shock of having heard what Justin was saying.

While they watched the beginners ride around the ring with more or less skill, Angelica said, "You first."

Heather told her how she had come into the stable and overheard Justin's phone conversation. "I think he was talking to the murderer," she said, getting goose bumps all over her body as she said it. "How could he be involved in something like this, when he seems so nice and kind? I'll never be able to trust a guy ever again!"

"Just wait, we'll find out both why and how!" Angelica stared toward the ring with a fierce expression on her face. Heather nodded silently. After a while, she said, "But how did *you* come to suspect Justin? It was something that happened yesterday, right? That's why you left so suddenly and wouldn't tell me why."

Angelica didn't answer right away. "I wasn't sure, so I didn't want to say anything. You like him so much, so I couldn't just come to you and rattle off a bunch of suspicions against him, right out of the blue."

She stopped for a moment before she continued. "Haven't you wondered why he was always so eager to convince you not to talk to the police, but to do exactly as the murderer was telling you to do?"

Heather nodded. "But I thought he did it to protect me," she said. "That it was because he was afraid something would happen to me."

"That's what I thought too, at first," said Angelica, "but then I started wondering. And yesterday he totally gave himself away,

66

and that's when I had to get out of there. I got so flustered I didn't know what to do."

"He gave himself away? How?" Heather looked confused. She couldn't remember Justin having said anything suspicious.

"He said you had been warned several times, both at the stable and at home. How did he know that you had received a warning note at home?"

Heather gaped at her. "You're right! At least I haven't told him about that."

"Me neither. So how could he have known?"

"He couldn't have," said Heather slowly, while the truth occurred to her, "unless..."

"Exactly!" Angelica looked at her triumphantly.

The brunt of the shock had started subsiding, and Heather could feel anger start rising inside her. "You just wait until that idiot, that two-faced jerk comes back," she said with stifled fury. "He's going to hear a piece of my mind!"

"Are you crazy? That would be madness! You mustn't say a word to him!"

"Why not?" Heather looked at her friend with exasperation. "Are you saying I should walk around pretending like nothing is wrong?"

"Yes, that's exactly what I'm saying." Angelica set her eyes at her. "If you talk to him now, he'll just deny everything and we'll have accomplished nothing. No, we need to be a lot smarter than that."

"What do you mean?"

"We have to set a trap for him, and when he goes in the trap, he'll have no choice. Then he'll have to tell us the truth. It's a good thing you didn't tell him that you remembered the murderer's face yesterday. We're going to take advantage of that now. You see, I've just come up with a fool-proof plan..."

Chapter 11

"Are you sure this is a smart thing to do?" said Heather, probably for the tenth time, looking around the stable with a worried look. It was late evening and the girls were alone in there with the horses. "Maybe it would be better to go to the police..."

Angelica just snorted. "It could take days for the police to catch the murderer based on your description. Even if they took us seriously and talked to Justin, he could just say he doesn't know a thing about it. And we have no evidence that he's involved. No, this is a much better idea. You remembered to tell him everything you were supposed to, right?"

Heather nodded. It hadn't been easy to act all unaware and natural around Justin when he showed up after his ride, but it didn't look like Justin noticed.

"He was probably paralyzed with fear when you told him how your memory had miraculously returned," snickered Angelica.

"That's exactly what I thought," said Heather, thinking back to the conversation she'd had with Justin.

"What do you mean?" he had said, clearly alarmed, when she told him she remembered everything.

"Just what I'm saying," answered Heather. "It all came back to me last night as I was about to go to sleep," she lied. "I was thinking about something else, and then suddenly I saw him in my inner eye. No cloud this time. So I can describe him to the police now, if I want to."

"You're not going to do that, are you?" Justin had looked so worried that if she hadn't known the reason, she would have felt sorry for him.

"I don't know what to do." Heather looked up at him, hoping she succeeded in looking helpless and innocent. "Angelica wants me to go to the police, but that's easy for her to say. It's not her horse who's at stake."

"No, it's not. Because if it was..." Justin went silent suddenly, a peculiar expression on his face. "I don't think you should do anything at all before you've thought it through really well," he said quickly. "Don't listen to Angelica. She doesn't know what she's talking about. She doesn't have a clue how dangerous it can be to know too much!"

Heather promised to think it over until the next day. "I'd rather not say anything at all," she'd told him before she and Justin parted. "But you know how bossy Angelica can be. It's not easy to stand up to all her nagging. If she goes to the police tomorrow and tells them that I've got my memory back..."

Heather hadn't said anything more. Justin left right after that. Heather watched him as he left the stable. Had he taken the bait? She couldn't tell.

At first Heather had refused to go along with Angelica's "brilliant" idea, but she had finally given in. And here she was, sitting in the stable. Heather sighed as she looked around the empty stall where she and Angelica had settled in for the night. Officially Angelica was supposedly sleeping over at Heather's house and vice versa.

The stall was furthest back in the stable. It was the only one that wasn't being used at the moment. Heather wished they could have been hiding in a stall closer to the door instead, in case they needed to retreat in a hurry.

"How do we know that Justin isn't dangerous?" whispered Heather as she looked at Angelica.

"You can't be absolutely sure about anything in life," said Angelica philosophically while stretching. "But I don't think we'll have any problems with him. After all, we're two against

69

one, and he's not exactly the biggest and strongest guy around..."

Heather looked at her with a horrified expression. The thought of having to fight Justin was so unappealing to her that she was speechless.

"Well, you can fight him then," she said sarcastically. "You're the one who's taken karate lessons. I'm not doing it, I can promise you that."

"Relax, said Angelica. "Of course we don't have to fight him. When he realizes that he's been caught red-handed, he'll collapse like a house of cards..."

Heather wished she were as confident as Angelica about that.

They waited for two everlasting hours before something finally happened. By then even Angelica was about to give up.

"Doesn't look like anything's going to happen," she complained. "He's not coming."

Heather hoped she was right. She didn't like this at all and just wanted to go home. Right now she didn't really care whether the murderer was caught or not.

But then they heard something. It was the sound of footsteps on the gravel outside.

Heather pinched Angelica in the arm. Her heart beat hard inside her, from anticipation and fear. The stable door was opened quietly and they could see the dark silhouette of a person against the night sky outside. Heather held her breath. More than ever, she wished that she were lying safely in her own bed at home. But now it was too late.

The girls were as quiet as mice, as he came walking down the hallway between the stalls. One of the horses snorted quietly and got up on his legs, curious about the nighttime visitor. He walked right past them, over to Crissy's stall.

The girls didn't dare move a muscle, for fear that he would hear them. It was important to wait for the right moment.

Heather heard him rummage around with something inside Crissy's stall. There was a sound of metal. What was he doing? He couldn't have a knife, could he? What if he hurt Crissy?

Heather glanced at Angelica and saw that the same thought had occurred to her, and suddenly she jumped up, rushed out of the stall and over to Crissy's stall. The sound of a shocked outburst came from there.

"What are you doing? What are you doing to my horse?" Angelica's voice was stifled.

Heather felt the urge to stay put where she was, safely hidden inside the empty stall. Angelica could probably manage this on her own. But the next moment she was ashamed by such cowardly thoughts and hurried out of the stall, following Angelica. Inside Crissy's stall stood Justin with a spray bottle in his hand. Some dark, thick fluid was running down Crissy's leg. Was it blood? Heather shuddered. This was not what they had expected. They had thought that Justin would show up and leave another warning note, nothing else.

"If you've hurt Crissy, I'll... I'll..." Angelica was so furious she couldn't find words. She shook her fists at Justin, who took a bewildered step back in shock.

Justin raised his hands to ward her off. "It... it's not dangerous... it's just red paint..." He lowered his head and looked down.

"I was just..." It looked like he realized that no lie would help him at this point, because he stopped.

"You were just going to leave another warning, isn't that right?" Angelica pointed an accusing finger at him. "A warning to make sure that I would be just as scared as Heather and stop nagging her about going to the police, right?"

Justin nodded. "I guess there's no point trying to deny it," he said quietly. "I'm actually kind of glad you caught me. This whole thing has been a nightmare from beginning to end. I'll tell you the whole story..." He lifted his head, looking straight at Heather. It was too dark for her to see the expression in his

71

eyes. What was he feeling right now? Anger? Shame? Regrets? She didn't know.

"What the heck are you dawdling for? Could you get a move on, so we can get out of here?!"

The voice made Heather jump. They had been so preoccupied with Justin and what was happening inside Crissy's stall that none of them had heard someone else enter the stable. Heather turned her head. For a moment it felt like her heart stopped completely, then it started beating at a furious speed. Even in the dim light inside the stall, she recognized him. The moment she had feared had arrived. She was face to face with the murderer, with no chance to escape. Right then Heather had forgotten that there were others in the stable. She stared at the man like she was hypnotized, expecting him to charge at her.

But the man seemed to have frozen to the spot just like Heather, the moment he realized that Justin wasn't alone in here.

"What the...?" He stopped himself, staring wildly at the three who were squished together inside Crissy's stall. "What are those girls doing here? I'll..."

He took a step toward them. Heather screamed and backed into the wall. Her legs quivered like jelly.

Suddenly Justin stood between her and the man. "What exactly will you do? Kill us all? Don't you see that the game is over? If you had just turned yourself in at once, you wouldn't..."

"Shut up!" roared the man. He put his hand to his head. "I've got to get away," he moaned. "Away!"

Then he turned and ran down the hallway.

"Wait!" called Justin. "It's no use running away, don't you see that? Why can't you just go to the police and tell them the truth? It was an accident! Dad, listen to me..."

But the man didn't stop; he ran out the door.

Heather clung to the bars in the wall. Justin had said "Dad"... She looked up at him. Justin stood there like a wax statue, without moving, looking toward the stable door.

72

"He's your dad?" Angelica's voice was incredulous.

Justin nodded. "Yes," he admitted slowly.

Heather's mind was total chaos. She opened her mouth to say something, but just then they heard voices shouting outside.

They ran to the window. "Over there," said Angelica, pointing.

Two men in dark clothes were dragging another man between them. It was Justin's dad.

"The police," said Justin. "Did you call them?"

"Us? No!" said Angelica. "We didn't have a clue that the murd... um, your dad, I mean, would come here."

A police car drove up. The two officers led Justin's father over to it. As they pushed him into the back seat, Justin turned away from the window.

"I might as well go out there before they come in after me," he said in a somber voice.

"But you haven't really done anything wrong," Heather blurted out.

"He hasn't?!" Angelica sounded shocked. "What about the threats?"

"The police don't know anything about that," argued Heather. She didn't know why she was defending Justin after what he'd done, but right then she just felt terribly sorry for him.

"They'll find out soon enough," said Justin over his shoulder. "I'm going to tell them everything, and then they can do whatever they want with me."

Heather and Angelica looked at each other. They didn't know what to say. They watched in silence as Justin went outside to the waiting police car.

73

Chapter 12

The next day Heather didn't make it to the stable until afternoon. First she had slept in kind of late, and then the police came by to talk to her about the previous night's events. They had been at Angelica's house and talked to her as well.

Heather was very curious about why the police happened to show up so conveniently the night before. The answer came as a total surprise to her.

"We've been keeping an eye on you for a couple of days now," one of the police officers explained. "You were an important witness, and both your mother and we thought you might be in danger. So we've been shadowing you as well as we could, without you knowing it. We didn't want to frighten you more than we had to."

Heather remembered the white car she had seen, the one she thought might be following her. That must have been the police then!

In broad daylight the night's happenings seemed like an unreal dream to Heather. She wondered how Justin was doing. Would he have to go to prison, like his dad? Did she wish he would? She didn't know.

"If you hurry up and get Caliban ready, we could go for a ride together," shouted Angelica when Heather parked her bike by the stable wall. She had already saddled up Crissy and was all ready to go. "I'll ride a few times around the ring while I wait for you," she called over her shoulder, while Heather scurried into the stable to get Caliban, who was waiting patiently.

"Hey, did you miss me?" Heather stroked him over the muzzle. He just snorted and shook his head. Heather wasn't sure how to read it. Maybe he was offended?

"I'm sorry I made you wait so long. A lot has happened, you see. But now we can go for a ride, you and I. You'll like that, won't you?"

Caliban turned his head and looked at her, as if he was saying, *Sure, sure, just get me out of here!* Heather laughed and went to get his saddle and bridle.

"Did you get in trouble with your mom when she found out where you had been last night?" asked Angelica curiously, as they were riding out from the stable yard a little later.

"Did I ever!" Heather shook her head. "You should have seen her when I came back in the middle of the night and woke her up. At first she thought that you and I had had a fight and that that was the reason I came rushing home like that. When I told her what had happened, I thought she was gonna go through the roof. I haven't seen her so mad since that time I poured liquid dish soap in the dishwasher and foamed up the entire kitchen all the way to the ceiling. Afterwards she started crying, and that was even worse."

Angelica nodded sympathetically. "My mom threw a fit too, when I told her. She bawled me out, saying we were stark, raving mad for doing something like that. Didn't we understand how dangerous it was, and so on and so on."

Heather shuddered. No, they had not understood how dangerous it could have been. What if Justin hadn't come at all, only his dad? If he was desperate enough... She didn't want to think about it. It had ended well, after all.

When the girls got back from their ride they had a surprise waiting for them. There was Justin, standing outside the stable. He looked up when they walked the horses into the stable yard.

75

Heather got a funny feeling inside. She didn't know whether to be furious with Justin or to feel sorry for him.

"Hi," he said quietly. "I came to talk to Betty, and wanted to talk to you too, before I leave town."

"Are you going away?" Heather looked at him.

Justin nodded. "I'll be staying with my grandmother for a few weeks, until things quiet down a bit. Betty promised to take care of Bogart while I'm gone."

"So the police let you go, then!" Angelica blurted out.

Justin blushed and lowered his head. "For now, yes," he said. "I don't know what will happen later."

Heather and Angelica tethered the horses outside the stable and sat down next to Justin. The stable yard was empty and quiet, as everybody else seemed to be at lessons or out on a ride.

When Justin started talking, Heather forgot everything else.

"You've probably heard that my parents are divorced," he said, prompting a nod from the girls. "But you may not know why. My mom found out that Dad was involved in some shady business dealings. She warned him several times, but he wouldn't listen, just kept talking about easy money and minimal risk. Finally, my mom had had enough, and left him."

Heather started seeing where this was going. "So your dad was involved in the bribes and everything that went on at Gold Enterprises?" she asked.

Justin nodded. "He was some kind of middle man, and had contact with John Simmons, among others. When the investigators started suspecting Mr. Simmons, he decided to reveal all his contacts. Dad found out about it and went to see Mr. Simmons, trying to use threats in order to get him to keep quiet. It evolved into a fight, and during the struggle Mr. Simmons fell and hit his head against something. At least that's what my dad claims and has been claiming all along –

76

that it was an accident that caused Mr. Simmons to die. I don't know if the police believe him."

"Do *you* believe him?" asked Heather defiantly. He didn't answer, but just looked down. Heather didn't know what to say. They sat quietly for a while, all three of them.

"But how did *you* get into the picture?" asked Angelica finally, wanting to break the awkward silence.

"The same way Heather did. And because I'm too curious for my own good," said Justin bitterly. "If I had minded my own business, I could have avoided a lot of trouble. But there's no use thinking about that now."

He shrugged his shoulders. "I was out riding when I saw Dad's car driving into the woods. Of course, I wondered what on earth he was doing there, so I followed him. I guess I thought he might be meeting someone there to exchange dirty money or something like that, but when I saw what he had in the trunk, I panicked and ran."

"Just like me," said Heather, nodding. "Talk about double trouble," she added. "First he's seen by his own son, and then by a stranger who comes riding by."

"He was scared out of his mind," said Justin. "He saw me as I rode away, so he came by and warned me to keep quiet. I begged him to turn himself in, but he went totally bananas and threatened to hurt Mom if I didn't do as he said. He also started talking about you, that you were a danger to him. I was terrified by the thought of what he might do. It was my idea to write those warning notes to persuade you to keep quiet. Of course, your memory loss helped a lot."

Heather nodded. No wonder Justin had been so eager to tell her how dangerous it could be to remember too much. What a hopeless situation he had gotten into.

"And so, when I started nagging Heather about going to the police, you decided to threaten me too, with Crissy." Angelica glanced at him. "Heather gave you the idea when she told you it was easy enough for me to talk about the police, as it was not my horse who had been threatened. Too bad you had already let it slip that you knew more about the warning notes than you should have."

Justin nodded again. "Yeah, I didn't have a clue that you guys were on to me," he said. "All I could think of was to keep my dad from hurting anyone. As long as I managed to convince him that you weren't going to the police, he was under control."

"I'm sorry about all the trouble it meant for you, but I'm really glad that your dad was caught," said Heather, placing her hand on his arm. He gave her a quick smile, and then he was serious again.

"If I could do the last few days over again, I'd do everything differently," he said. "I should never have agreed to cover up for him, but I was so confused. I didn't know what to do. He's my dad, after all!"

Justin got up and got ready to leave. "I hope you can forgive me some day," he said, looking straight at Heather.

Heather didn't answer, because she didn't know what to say.

Justin's shoulders drooped as he walked toward his bike.

"I'll see you when you get back," Heather called after him. "Let's just see what happens. I need some time to think."

He looked back at her with a quick, slanted smile before biking away. Heather watched him. Then she turned toward the wall to hide the tears in her eyes. Would she ever be able to forgive Justin? Yeah, she thought so. But was she still in love with him? She wasn't sure; her feelings were all in a jumble right now. She took a deep breath and turned toward Angelica.

"You know what?" she said. "For the rest of this vacation, I don't even want to look at a boy. They're just loads of trouble."

Angelica laughed. "Now, don't go promising more than you can keep," she teased. "But I'm with you. Who needs boys when we can be around the most fantastic creatures in the whole world? And the best of it is, they don't ever betray you."

She walked over to Crissy and ruffled her mane.

"That's right, and they don't lie to you either," agreed Heather. She decided to put Justin out of her mind for now. She'd just have to see how she felt about him when he came back. But until then...

She hurried over to Caliban. "From now on, you'll be my only boyfriend, just so you know," she said, stroking him over the ridge of his nose. Caliban snorted contentedly as he gave her shoulders a playful push with his muzzle. Heather laid her face into the warm, safe head of her horse, feeling peace spread throughout her body. The nightmare was finally over.

Part 2
The Thief

Chapter 1

"Only one week to go, and this dream will end!" Angelica turned around with a gloomy look at Heather.

The girls were taking a ride together. Heather sat on Caliban's back and didn't know what to say. She was perfectly aware of how lucky she was to have her own horse. She patted Caliban on the neck as she glanced over at Angelica. Her friend was riding Crissy, whom she had taken care of for a whole year now. Heather remembered the day when Angelica came running to tell her the good news, how absolutely thrilled she had been. It was hard to believe that a whole year had gone by already. But it had, and next week Anna was due to come and get her horse. No wonder Angelica was depressed.

"I wish I could buy Crissy," said Angelica with a sigh. "But you know how it is; I might as well be wishing for the moon!"

Heather nodded. Poor Angelica! By now she loved Crissy every bit as much as Heather loved Caliban. Heather looked sympathetically at her friend. She could easily imagine what this must be like for her. If she had had to give up Caliban in a week... she shuddered at the thought and found it too unpleasant to even entertain the idea.

"But enough of this gloominess!" said Angelica suddenly. "I will not destroy these last few days I have left with Crissy. I want to enjoy every second to the fullest, until Anna comes and tows her away."

She pointed at a tree some distance away. "Last one to the big pine tree is a rotten egg!"

Heather spurred Caliban into a gallop, but had no chance of

catching up with Angelica, who had given herself a solid head start.

"You, cheater!" laughed Heather as she arrived at the tree where Angelica was waiting. "You were halfway across the field before I could even start."

"Was not!" snorted Angelica. "A few yards, maybe..."

She stopped. "Look who's coming," she said, pointing.

Heather followed her gaze and her heart made a jump as she caught sight of the rider who was heading toward them. Justin! Heather's mouth felt dry all of a sudden. She had heard he was back in town, but hadn't really expected to see him this soon.

Just then, Justin caught sight of them as well. He reined his horse in and for a moment it looked as if he was about to turn around. But then he continued riding toward them slowly.

Heather's mind went back to the awful days of last summer. She only needed to close her eyes and she was back in the woods, hearing the sound of someone digging.

"Hi!"

His voice pulled Heather back to the present. She looked at him. He was exactly like she remembered him; he hadn't changed a bit.

Heather opened her mouth to say something, but couldn't make a sound. Fortunately Angelica was better able to speak.

"Hello there," she said with a smile to Justin. "Long time no see. How are you doing?"

"Fine, thanks," mumbled Justin. He seemed shy and ill at ease.

"Heather and I were wondering what happened to you. We thought you'd come back for school, but you didn't."

Justin shook his head. "No, I couldn't stand the thought of it. I could just picture how everyone would be pointing and whispering behind my back. 'Look, there's the son of the murderer', and so on. My mom agreed, and so did the people in Children's Services. They got involved after the police were done questioning me."

84

Justin shrugged his shoulders. "I stayed with my grandparents this school year, which wasn't so bad. But now I'm hoping it'll be okay to move back home."

He looked at Heather with a question in his eyes, and it occurred to her that he was wondering if she was still angry and bitter at him for what had happened. Heather wasn't really sure how she felt, but she was willing to give Justin a new chance. She smiled at him and gave him a thumbs up. He smiled back, clearly relieved.

"I bet you're glad to be back with Bogart," she said, nodding toward his horse. "You must have missed him terribly!"

Bogart had been boarded at Stardust Stable the whole time Justin had been gone. Betty had kept him there at no charge, in exchange for getting to use him as a school horse when needed.

"Not just Bogart," said Justin quietly.

Heather felt herself blush. Was he saying that he had missed her? She didn't quite know what to think.

"Do you think we could be friends again?" Justin looked uncertainly from Heather to Angelica.

Heather hesitated for a moment, and then nodded slowly. "Of course we can," she said.

"Well, if Heather can forgive you, who'm I to do less?" said Angelica quickly. "Let's start over, and forget what happened. Heather and I were going for a ride to the lake. Do you want to come?"

Justin shook his head. "That would have been great," he said, "thanks, but I have an appointment with Betty. I have to talk to her about Bogart and stable room and all that. If I need stable room, that is," he said so quietly that the girls almost didn't hear him.

"What do you mean?" Heather looked at him with big eyes. "Why wouldn't you need stable room for your horse?"

Justin looked down, while Bogart was stomping his feet,

waiting impatiently to get going. It seemed to rub off on Caliban because Heather could barely hold him back.

"I may have to sell Bogart."

"What? Why?" Angelica stared at him in disbelief.

"Money matters," answered Justin, downhearted. "After Dad went to prison, it's been harder for my mom to make ends meet. He used to pay a fair amount of child support, you know, but now he can't. So it's up in the air whether I can keep Bogart or not."

The girls watched him as he slowly rode back to the riding school. Poor Justin! First all the problems with his dad, and now this. Heather got a lump in her throat. She hoped things would turn out all right for Justin.

"There's one thing you haven't managed during this year with Crissy," giggled Heather as she directed Caliban into the water. "You didn't cure her of her fear of the water!"

Angelica sat at the edge of the water while Crissy carefully stretched a hoof toward the scary, wet, mirror-like surface in front of her. Did she dare? Maybe. If Caliban could do it, maybe it wasn't so bad. But before her hoof hit the water, Crissy changed her mind, backed up a couple of steps and planted her hooves on the ground. And there she remained. Her body language was very clear: This far, and not a step further!

Heather laughed out loud, because Crissy reminded her of a stubborn little toddler. Just then there was a gust of wind sweeping across the water. The wind carried with it a white plastic bag. Heather didn't see it until it fluttered right in front of Caliban's head. Neither did he, so he got really spooked, gave a loud neigh and reared up. It all happened so suddenly and unexpected that before Heather knew it she landed in the water with a splash. This time it was Angelica's turn to laugh. She was lying forward in the saddle, laughing hysterically at

86

her dripping wet friend, who led Caliban back up on the shore and was struggling to get back in the saddle.

"Aren't you going to empty your boots?" gasped Angelica. "What if there's fish in them? Oh, I think I'm gonna die. You have no idea how funny you looked when you landed in the water."

"I don't think it's the least bit funny," hissed Heather, but as she looked down at herself, she had to laugh too.

It was an uncomfortable ride back to the stable, in soaked clothes and heavy boots that made gurgling sounds. Heather had been hoping to sneak out of there before anybody saw her, because she didn't want to hear any more humorous comments about the condition she was in. But when they rode into the stable yard, Betty showed up, and Heather had to tell her what happened. Betty got a good laugh out of it as well.

"You'd better run home and change your clothes," she said. "And stuff your riding boots with newspaper or something like that – then they'll be dry in no time."

Heather nodded. "I'll just fix some food for Caliban first."

Betty turned to Angelica. "I've got some bad news," she started. "Anna just called..."

"Oh, no! Don't tell me she's coming for Crissy already!" Angelica gave Betty a distraught look.

Betty shook her head. "No, no, quite the contrary. She's not coming for a while yet. She went skiing on a glacier in Austria or somewhere and broke her leg. Hence Crissy will be here for at least another couple of months."

"That's what you call bad news?" Angelica practically jumped for joy in the saddle.

"Well, yes, bad news for Anna, that is." Betty was shaking her head. "But I can see that you don't have much sympathy for the poor girl."

Angelica stopped her cheering and got serious. "I'm sorry!" she said. "I didn't mean any harm. It's just that... that …"

87

"… That you get to keep Crissy for the whole summer," Betty finished the sentence for her. She smiled. "Oh, I understand you. Of course you're happy about that. But do think about Anna a little too, please. She had been looking forward to riding her horse during her vacation."

Betty went into the stable, and the girls followed her with the horses.

"Poor Anna, I really do feel sorry for her," said Angelica, meaning it. "It must be pretty awful to be bumping around on crutches all summer and not be able to do anything fun. Please give her our best wishes, Betty. I promise to take extra good care of Crissy."

"I don't doubt that," said Betty with a little dry sarcasm. She reached her hand out toward the stall on her right. Red Ron, a beautiful, chestnut gelding, eagerly stuck his muzzle out toward her, wanting to be patted.

"And this handsome chap will be leaving us soon," she said, scratching his forehead.

"Really? Why?" asked Heather and Angelica in unison.

"He'll never be a good stable school horse. I can see that now." Betty sighed. "I made a mistake buying him, I'm afraid, but I didn't realize how unruly and hard he would be to handle. The seller managed to pull the wool over my eyes."

"You're not having him put down, are you?" Heather gave Betty a shocked look.

"Oh no, you can take it easy. I've received a good offer from a lady I know. Her name is Amanda. We've done business with each other before. Amanda thinks that Red Ron is showing great jumping talent, and she might be right. But I'm going to miss this rascal." She ruffled the horse's mane.

"Amanda is coming some day next week. She's a very special lady. Stubborn as a mule if something doesn't suit her. Last time she was here, she bought a foal from me. That time she showed up with a bag full of money, insisting on paying for the horse in cash. I wouldn't be surprised if she does the same thing this time. I just hope she doesn't get robbed some day. I keep telling her that, but she just laughs at me, saying I'll never see the day when she gets talked into using a check or bank card. It's madness, if you ask me."

Betty shook her head as she turned and went back to her office. All of a sudden Justin came out of Bogart's stall. Heather hadn't noticed him before. Had he been there the whole time?

She gave him a shy smile, and he smiled back.

"Oh hey, I almost forgot." Betty turned around in the doorway of her office and looked at them. "Thursday is the deadline for paying the deposit for the riding camp at the end of July. I assume you'll be coming, all three of you?"

"Of course! I've been saving up for months for that camp. And now I can even take Crissy along. That's even better than I had hoped for! I can't wait." Angelica beamed at Betty. "How much was the deposit again?"

"A hundred and fifty dollars. And then another hundred and fifty to be paid a week before the camp starts. That includes transportation of the horses."

"Um, I'll have to see if I can sign up or not. I'm not sure I'll have the time to go." Justin squirmed and looked like he wished he could disappear.

"Well, just make up your mind by Thursday at the latest," said Betty. "I hope you can make it. It'll be a real wilderness camp with lots of fun."

She went into her office, closing the door behind her.

Justin stood there with a dismal expression on his face. Then he suddenly said goodbye to Heather and Angelica and left the stable.

Heather watched him go. She felt so sorry for Justin. He probably couldn't afford to go to the summer camp. Betty should have understood that. But maybe she wasn't aware of how difficult the money situation was at Justin's house right now.

Heather shrugged her shoulders and went into Caliban's stall. He rubbed his head against her sweater, which was still uncomfortably damp. She scratched him behind the ears and made some small talk before she finally biked home to get changed into some dry clothes. By then she had forgotten all about Justin and his problems.

Chapter 2

Heather was warm and out of breath when she parked her bike outside the stable the next morning. First she had overslept, and then her mom started interrogating her about Justin. Heather regretted having been stupid enough to mention to her mom that he was back.

Her mom was not at all happy about Heather and Justin being friends again.

"I know it might be unfair of me," she said, while distractedly lifting the teacup to her mouth and putting it back down without drinking any. "But he did help his dad by threatening you, after all. And I'm just afraid there's a reason we have the saying 'like father, like son.' People are not always as nice and honest as they may seem on the surface. I ought to know, having worked for that smooth-spoken Mr. Simmons for several years without having a clue about what kind of scoundrel he really was."

Her mom went on and on, but Heather was no longer listening. She knew the story by heart already.

"... And therefore I think you should be careful and keep your distance."

"Huh?" Heather looked up and met her mom's gaze.

"You never listen when I talk to you!" Her mom sighed irritably. "I'm just saying that even though Justin might actually be a nice and honest boy, I think that for now you should look before you leap and keep him at a distance. After what happened last year, I just can't bring myself to trust him yet."

"All right! I'll keep in mind what you've said," Heather promised and scurried out the door before her mom could get started on something else. Good thing her dad had gone to work already, or she would probably have gotten the warning in stereo mode, she thought as she arrived a short while later at the stable and started the morning routine.

Caliban greeted her with a loud neigh. He was clearly hungry. Heather quickly got some hay for him. She had to smile at the way he avidly threw himself at the food, as if he had been starving for days.

"You sure are sweet, even if you make a fuss," she said, patting him on the neck. Caliban didn't pay any attention to her. He had more important things to do.

"Hi! I almost started thinking you weren't going to show up today!"

Heather turned and saw Angelica. She was standing in the hallway with a girl Heather hadn't seen before.

"Mom was giving a lecture. I'll tell you later." Heather looked curiously at the new girl.

"Oh, I'm sorry; this is Keisha," said Angelica. "She just moved to town and will be taking riding lessons here. Betty asked me to show her around."

"Hi!" said Keisha, smiling a little shyly. "I'm so glad I found this stable. It seems like a really nice place. And the horses are beautiful. Especially that dark one over there." She pointed.

"His name is Bogart," informed Angelica. "Justin, the boy who owns him, will probably show up soon, and then you can meet him too."

"Too bad Bogart is a private horse," said Keisha, looking longingly at the handsome horse. "Otherwise I might have been able to buy him. Grandpa has promised that I'll get my own horse if I can find one that's suitable and doesn't cost too much. That was one of his bribes in order to convince me to move here. My dad died in an accident a year ago, and after that my mom couldn't really keep our old house anymore."

Keisha looked sad for a moment, and then she smiled again.

"But now I can't see why I was so against moving. Mom was absolutely thrilled at my grandpa's suggestion, but I didn't want to go, even though..."

Keisha stopped and the sad expression was there again. Heather was thinking she probably missed her dad. She meant to ask what kind of accident he'd been in, but right then Justin showed up and Angelica called his name and waved him over.

Justin came over to them and said hi to Keisha, who instantly started praising Bogart.

"Too bad he's not for sale," she said laughingly. "I would have bought him in an instant if I could."

Justin's expression darkened and he mumbled that he'd better get started on his morning work. Keisha looked bewildered as he walked away in abrupt strides.

"I hope he didn't get mad," she said timidly. "Did I say something wrong?"

"Don't worry about it," said Angelica kindly. "How could you know that Justin might have to sell Bogart?"

Keisha looked inquiringly at her. Angelica glanced at Heather, who shrugged her shoulders.

"Since you're going to be coming to the stable anyway, you might as well know," said Angelica. Then she told Keisha briefly about what had happened the previous year.

"Justin has just returned and has started coming to the stable again, and it's clear that he and his mom have some financial problems," finished Angelica.

Keisha nodded with a contemplative expression on her face. "So he may be forced to sell his horse. No wonder he got upset at what I said. I really hope he doesn't have to sell Bogart, even though I wish he was mine. He's an absolutely gorgeous horse!"

"So he is!" said Betty, who was just passing by. "But there are plenty of other good horses in the area, so I'm sure we can find a suitable one for you. Your grandfather has asked me to help you look for a good horse. You're sure lucky to have such a kind and generous grandfather."

Keisha nodded, but Heather didn't really think she looked very happy. It looked like something was bothering her. But then Keisha gave a beaming smile again and started talking about how she looked forward to riding in the pretty area around the riding school. Heather decided that she must have just imagined an unhappy look on Keisha's face.

"Betty said I can rent one of the school horses until I find a horse to buy," said Keisha. "You guys probably know most of the horses. Which one should I choose?"

"That depends on your level of riding skills," said Angelica.

"Well, I'd hardly win any championships," said Keisha slowly. "But I've been riding for quite a while and know all the basics. I think I could handle most horses, as long as they're not too stubborn or rowdy. And I do like a good gallop, so I wouldn't want a horse who's so old and slow that I'd be riding along in slow motion."

"Ask Betty if you can use Tinto," said Angelica. "He's pretty spunky, but nice and easy at the same time. I'm pretty sure you'll like Tinto."

"Then I'll go and ask her right away," said Keisha and headed to the office.

She came back almost before she had gone inside.

"I'd better learn to knock before I barge in on people," she said, shaking her head.

"Why?" Heather looked confusedly at her. "Betty doesn't usually care if we knock or not."

"Oh, I think she would care this time," said Keisha, "if she had seen me, that is." She started giggling. "I opened the door and there was Betty with a man. They were glued together, kissing. I just quickly backed out and closed the door again. I don't think they noticed. They seemed pretty caught up in each other."

"Argh, so Kenny is here again!" Heather made a grimace. "I don't know what Betty sees in that guy."

Betty's new boyfriend was a salesman who traveled a lot for his job. What exactly he was selling, Heather didn't know. And to be honest, she didn't really care to know either.

"That's not fair, Heather!" Angelica looked crossly at her. "I don't see what you have against the man! He's been nothing but nice and friendly, as far as I've seen."

Heather shrugged her shoulders, not knowing what to say. Angelica was right. Kenny had always acted friendly toward Heather. Even so, she just didn't like him. Maybe it was because he didn't like horses? But people could be nice, even if they didn't like animals.

"Maybe you're right, it's probably me there's something wrong with," said Heather to end the discussion. "Maybe it's that slick salesman charm that I have a problem with. The important thing, of course, is that Betty likes him. So what does it matter if I don't?"

As they spoke the office door opened and Kenny and Betty came out. They exchanged a few words, and then Kenny waved cheerfully at the girls and left the stable. Betty went back into her office.

"Now you can go and ask Betty about Tinto," said Angelica, nudging Keisha in the back. "After that pleasant interlude she'll probably be in a great mood and will give you whatever you want."

"I hope you're right," giggled Keisha as she walked toward the office.

Angelica watched her go. Then she turned to Heather. "I hope you don't mind if she comes riding with us," she said. "I felt like I had to ask her. She doesn't know anybody in the stable yet."

Heather shook her head. "No, that's fine with me. Keisha seems pretty nice, so we'll probably have a good time together.

Maybe we should ask a couple of the other girls as well, to give Keisha a chance to get to know them."

"Good idea! I'll go and see who's still around." Angelica walked down the hallway.

Heather went to the saddle room to get Caliban's saddle and bridle. As she got close to the door, she heard Justin's voice on the inside. She hesitated in the doorway, peeking inside first. Justin was standing in the back of the room with his back turned toward her. He was talking on his cell phone.

"Yes, yes, I've already told you I can come up with it, so just relax!" Justin sounded irritated. "A.s.a.p., I know!"

Heather cleared her throat as she entered the room. Justin glanced at her, and then he said goodbye to the person he was talking to and hung up.

"Are you going for a ride?" he asked.

Heather nodded. "We're taking Keisha along, the new girl, so she can get acquainted with the area. I don't suppose you'd like to come along, and play rooster in the chicken coop?"

Justin grinned and shook his head. "No, thanks anyway," he said. "Maybe some other time. Right now I don't have the time. I have something to take care of."

Heather wondered what Justin was up to, while she saddled up Caliban. But a little while later, when she was riding down the trail with the other girls, all thoughts of Justin were pushed from her mind. The air was fresh and crisp, the birds were chirping from the treetops and Caliban was in great spirits. He walked briskly underneath her, and she relished the feeling of being one with the horse.

This is the life, she thought lazily. Summer vacation, the best horse in the world, and nothing pressing to worry about. No homework for several weeks. Wonderful!

It was almost like Angelica had read her mind, because suddenly she said, "I don't envy Betty, having to work so hard on a nice day like this. She has riding lessons going continuously today, she told me."

"I sometimes think it would be nice to work with horses," said Keisha. "But maybe it would be smarter to just use them for fun. If we had to work with them day in and day out, maybe some of the charm would be gone, do you think?"

"I'm not so sure about that," said Angelica. "Just look at Betty. She has worked with horses for many years, and she's just as excited about them as ever."

Heather didn't feel like joining in the conversation. She listened distractedly to what the others were saying, more focused on enjoying Caliban and the ride. After a while the voices from the others became more like a distant hum that didn't involve her, and not until she was suddenly awakened by a frightened scream did she come to and look around. It was Keisha who had screamed. She was lying on the ground moaning. Heather felt cold inside. Was Keisha seriously hurt?

But fortunately she sat up, while rubbing her elbow and grinning with pain. Tinto was standing a short distance away looking totally innocent, as if he didn't have a clue how his rider had been thrown off his back.

"How are you?" asked Angelica concerned.

"Not too bad, I think." Keisha tried to get up, but fell back to the ground again. "Ouch! I think I must have sprained my ankle, and the elbow is pretty bruised. But other than that, I'm fine."

"What happened exactly?"

"I have no idea." Keisha shook her head. "I must not have paid attention for a moment. Tinto suddenly jumped to the side, and there I was on the ground. It was my own fault. I should have been more observant."

Keisha struggled to get back on her feet. She tried to put some weight on the injured ankle. It worked, but was apparently very painful because she was making faces and got tears in her eyes.

"I think I'd better go home," she said miserably.

97

"We'll go with you," offered Angelica.

Keisha shook her head. "No, that's not necessary. If you can just help me back in the saddle, I know the way. I just stay on this trail back to the big rock and then turn left, right?"

Heather nodded. "That's right. You can't get lost as long as you stay on the trail. But are you sure you don't want us to go with you? It's no problem at all."

But Keisha didn't want that. "This was just my own stupid mistake," she said. "There's no reason you guys should have your ride interrupted because of me. I'll be fine, and I promise I'll pay attention to what I'm doing on the way back."

They watched Keisha as she headed back the way they had come.

"That's too bad," said Heather when Keisha was out of earshot. "I hope she hasn't broken anything. Then she wouldn't be able to ride for weeks."

"I don't think it's that serious," stated Angelica. "She's probably just somewhat bruised and battered. I bet she'll be back to normal in a day or two."

"I hope you're right," said Heather relieved. "What should we do now? Do you want to ride over to the big field by the pond? It's so nice to gallop there, and we can even make a hurdle if we want to."

Nobody had any objections to Heather's suggestion and the rest of the ride turned out just as fun as Heather had hoped. It looked like the horses really enjoyed the opportunity to gallop too, and afterwards they jumped some low nature hurdles that the girls gathered together. Caliban did the hurdles really well, prompting Heather to praise him. He flapped his ears and looked like he was enjoying the attention.

A few hours later they were a tired but contented gang who headed back to the riding school, ignorant of the drama that awaited them there.

Chapter 3

"Look, there's Betty!" said Angelica as the girls rode into the farmyard in front of the stable. "She probably just finished the last riding lesson."

Betty waved to them. "What a bunch of lazy bums, getting to ride around for fun while others have to work hard," she said, wiping sweat off her face. But she was smiling as she said it, so the girls knew she was just teasing them.

"Did you have a good ride?"

The girls told her excitedly about everything they had done. Betty got worried when she heard about Keisha's accident, but after a quick trip into the stable, she came back looking relieved.

"Tinto is safely back in his stall. I didn't see Keisha anywhere, so I assume she's gone home to rest or maybe to the clinic to get her ankle looked at. Apparently she managed to take off Tinto's saddle and bridle, so she couldn't be too badly injured. That's a relief. I'm glad she got back okay, and I don't want to rain on your parade when you've had such a good time and all. But the next time someone falls off a horse and gets hurt, I'd like you to please escort them back to the stable, just to be on the safe side. You could ride back out again afterward. This time it went well, but some other time it may not. People are often more hurt than they realize at first, and then things can go very wrong if they're sent home on their own."

"We'll remember that," said Angelica. "We did offer to go with her, but she didn't want us to."

"Just relax, no harm done," said Betty. "Just make sure that in the future at least one person escorts the injured rider back, even if the person who has fallen off and gotten hurt thinks it's embarrassing and would rather manage on their own."

The girls nodded to show that they understood.

"Well, I better get back to my never-ending paperwork!" Betty rolled her eyes as she sighed. "If this job was all about horses, life would be perfect. The person who invented bookkeeping should be exiled to a deserted island, along with their spread-sheets! But I might as well jump to it... see you later!"

She went into her office. A moment later there was a loud outburst in there, saying, "What in the world!" Betty appeared in the doorway. She was holding the moneybox. It was open and completely empty!

"I can't understand who would have taken the money!" Angelica was upset.

It was an hour later, and Heather and Angelica were standing in their separate stalls brushing dusty horse legs.

"I don't either." Heather shook her head. "Who on earth would do a thing like that to Betty? I mean, sure it wasn't a real fortune or anything, but four hundred and fifty dollars is certainly money! I don't think Betty is loaded with money exactly, so I'm sure she needs every penny."

"Well, who doesn't?" said Angelica dejectedly. "Now I'm glad I hadn't gotten around to paying the deposit for the summer camp yet. I meant to take care of it today, but I forgot my bank card at home so I couldn't withdraw the money."

"I guess Betty should be glad so many of us apparently wait until the last day to pay. If everybody had paid their deposits already, she might have lost a much bigger amount."

Heather yanked the comb through a stubborn tangle on Caliban's heel. He jolted and snorted irritably.

"I'm sorry, did that tickle?" She patted him soothingly on the neck, and he settled down.

"It wasn't very smart of Betty to ask for cash either," stated

Angelica. "Why didn't she just have us transfer the money into her account, like we did last time?"

"I heard that she's in the process of switching banks. Maybe that's why." Heather scratched Caliban on the forehead while thinking. "It might be too much trouble if people were trying to transfer money into an account that didn't exist anymore, or which had just been closed. I don't know. I don't really know anything about money, except that I never have enough of it!"

"Welcome to the club! I haven't met anybody yet who's said they have enough money."

The girls worked quietly for a while. The only sounds to be heard were scraping hooves and teeth munching on delicious hay.

"I wonder if Keisha might have seen something suspicious, since she came back to the stable before us," speculated Heather.

"And Justin was still in the stable when we left. Maybe he saw something. But probably not." Angelica shook her head. "If I were going to sneak into the office to steal money, I would've waited until I was sure nobody else was around."

They were interrupted by Betty, who showed up again. She was both agitated and sad.

"What a gyp!" she said. "I called the police and told them what happened, but would they come? Oh no. Since there was no 'breaking and entering', only theft, it's up to me to go down to the station to make a report."

Betty threw her arms out with a resigned look. "I guess I'd better do it, even though there's probably no point. I'm sure it won't do much good to contact the insurance company either. Most likely, they'll refuse to pay for damages because the door wasn't locked. To think I could be so stupid and careless! But I've never had any thefts in the stable before, so it didn't occur to me that I should be locking the office door."

She gave a sigh as she looked dismally off into space. "I'd

101

better talk to everybody who was here yesterday to check if anyone saw any strangers sneaking around."

"How do you know it was a stranger? Maybe it was somebody in the stable who needed money?" The comment came from Lisa, one of the girls in the stable. She had been standing nearby and had evidently heard what Betty said.

"No, I don't believe that for a second." Betty sounded utterly shocked. "Who would that be?"

Lisa squirmed. "No, I… I just thought… well, we all know that Justin is hard up for money, so maybe he…"

She didn't get to finish before Betty interrupted her. "Stop it! You can't go around accusing people of stealing for no reason! How would you like it if somebody said that about you?"

Lisa blushed and looked like she wished she could vanish. "I'm sorry!" she said, "But…"

"No buts!" Betty sounded angry. "I won't have people spreading malicious gossip about others around here. Is that clear?"

Lisa nodded and looked uneasy.

"And that goes for the rest of you who heard this too," said Betty looking around the stable. Nobody said a word. Betty shook her head as she turned and went back to her office. *She's perfectly aware that the gossip will spread regardless of what she said*, thought Heather as she watched her go.

The thought of Justin had actually occurred to Heather as well, but she had pushed it away. She couldn't help wondering if Lisa was right in her suspicions, though.

Suddenly Heather recalled the phone conversation she had overheard. Justin had promised to come up with something. What if he'd been talking about money? With a pang of guilt she realized she was doing the same thing Lisa had. She had no reason to think that Justin was the thief. Betty was probably right; it could just as easily have been a stranger who had been snooping around for some easy money.

102

Heather glanced at her watch. It was time to go home. She said goodbye to Angelica and put away her grooming tools. Tomorrow the case may be solved and the thief caught, she told herself as she biked home. But deep down she didn't really believe that.

Chapter 4

The next morning the stable was buzzing with gossip and rumors. Everybody had heard about the theft, and they all had a theory about what had happened and who was behind it. Most of them were sure that Justin was the culprit.

"Of course, somebody who's willing to help cover up a murder wouldn't think twice about a little stealing," Heather heard a girl say as she walked into the stable.

"And everybody knows that he needs money in order to keep his horse!" Lisa's shrill voice could be heard throughout the stable. "Isn't it obvious that..."

"I thought you promised Betty not to spread gossip left and right!" Heather glared accusingly at Lisa.

Lisa stared angrily back at her. She was red in the face. "I can't believe that you would defend him," she said, with her head in the air. "Have you forgotten what he did to you and Caliban? If it had been my horse..."

"But it wasn't, was it? And besides, Justin was forced to do what he did, which I think you know!"

Lisa opened her mouth to say something, but at that moment Justin showed up in the doorway. Everybody in the stable fell silent. Nobody quite knew what to say or do. Justin clearly understood that they had been talking about him, because he stiffened and suddenly looked uncomfortable. Without looking at anyone, he walked over to Bogart's stall, opened the door and disappeared behind his horse.

The girls standing in the hallway looked uncertainly at each other. Heather threw one last look of warning toward Lisa.

Then she proceeded to take care of Caliban, who was scraping his hooves impatiently, waiting for his breakfast.

Angelica came by and said hi. Heather waved her into the stall and told her in a whisper what had taken place and how they were gossiping about Justin.

"Let's hope the real thief is caught soon," said Angelica. "Otherwise it'll be impossible for Justin to keep coming to the stable."

Heather nodded. *But what if it was Justin?* a voice said inside her. She felt ashamed by her own thoughts, but couldn't totally rid herself of them. Fortunately Keisha showed up, which gave her something else to think about.

"Hi! Are you back already? How's it going?"

"I'm fine." Keisha smiled. "My elbow hurts a little, but it's not that bad. The ankle is almost completely well again. It was pretty swollen yesterday, so I could barely get off my riding boots after I got home. But this morning the swelling was almost gone, so I'm ready to ride again. Did you guys have a nice ride?"

"Great. I'm sorry you missed it."

"Apparently I missed more than the ride." Keisha motioned toward the stable door. Lisa and three other girls were standing there, eagerly whispering to each other.

"If I heard it right, Justin has stolen a bunch of money from Betty. Is it true?"

Angelica shook her head. "Don't believe everything that gossipy gang over there is saying. It's true that somebody has stolen four hundred and fifty dollars from Betty's moneybox. But nobody knows who did it. They're just suspecting Justin because of what happened last year, and because he has money problems."

Keisha threw a glance toward the stall where Bogart was standing. "Well, maybe it was Justin," she said ponderingly. "If Bogart had been my horse and I was in danger of losing him, I would be desperate enough to do just about anything to keep him."

Heather felt a knot in her stomach. What Keisha was saying did not at all sound unlikely. But no... she mustn't think like that... She gave a start when Betty's voice suddenly reverberated through the stable.

"Justin, would you come into my office after you're done grooming, please? I need to talk to you about Bogart."

Angelica, Heather and Keisha looked at each other. None of them really believed that Bogart was the reason Betty wanted to talk to Justin. Probably nobody else thought so either. When Justin went into Betty's office, the buzzing of voices reached a new level. The gossip was now running rampant between the stalls.

"Betty must have found him out..."

"He'll probably be banished from the stable for good..."

"Do you think the police will come and take him away?"

The door to the office opened and the whispering stopped instantly. Justin walked through the hallway without looking left or right. His face looked resentful and closed. Heather tried to catch his attention as he walked by her, but she might as well have been invisible. He went straight to Bogart's stall, saddled up the horse and led him outside. A moment later they could hear the clatter of hooves. Then horse and rider were gone.

Angelica and Heather looked at each other.

"I think we should ride after him and try to talk to him," said Angelica.

"I agree. This must be terrible for him, the way everybody is talking behind his back." Heather hurriedly went to get Caliban's saddle and bridle. She felt a pang of guilt. Who was she to criticize the others for gossiping? She was thinking the same thing herself. *But at least I haven't said it out loud*, she thought, in an attempt at defending herself.

Caliban could tell that she was nervous and in a hurry as she was getting him ready, and reacted by being totally uncooperative. Heather almost gave up trying to get the bit in his mouth, but finally he parted his teeth enough that she managed to get it in place.

"Stop being so difficult," she whispered to him. Caliban looked at her with such an innocent look that she had to smile. *Difficult? Who? Me?* he seemed to be saying.

"Yes, you!" said Heather, giving him a smack on the neck. Then she led him out to the stable yard, where Keisha and Angelica were waiting.

"I give up!" Angelica wiped a hand across her forehead and looked at her watch. "We've looked for them for over an hour without seeing so much as a shadow of Bogart and Justin. I can't understand where they went."

"Only five more minutes," Heather said. "Let's try that trail over there. If we don't see him before we reach the pond, then we'll stop."

They hadn't ridden for more than a couple of minutes when Keisha suddenly said, "Over there, Isn't that a horse?"

Heather shaded her eyes. Yes, it looked like a horse. They rode closer. Bogart was standing by a cluster of trees. Justin was sitting in the grass staring off into space with a gloomy expression. He didn't answer when they called his name.

Angelica turned to Heather. "Why don't you go and talk to him alone? We'll ride a little further. C'mon Keisha."

Keisha looked like she wanted to object, but then she shrugged her shoulders and went along with Angelica.

Heather tethered Caliban to a tree and walked over to Justin. He didn't look at her. She sat down in the grass next to him but didn't know what to say.

They sat in silence for a while. Then Justin said suddenly, "You probably think it was me too, don't you?"

Heather was taken aback by his direct question. What should she answer? Justin continued before she could say anything at all. Once he'd gotten started, it was as if a dam broke. The words poured out of him.

"I know what they're all saying about me. That I'm as good as a murderer and that obviously I'm a thief too. Betty thinks it's me too. I can see it in her eyes, even though she's trying to hide it. I'm not so stupid that I don't understand that I'm the obvious suspect. I was in the stable after the others had ridden out, and I could easily have gone into the office without anybody seeing me. But I swear to you, I didn't touch any money!"

Heather had never seen a more despairing look than the one he gave her then. A jolt went through her body, and most of all she wanted to put her arms around him. But she didn't do that. Instead she put her hand gently on his and said quietly, "If you're innocent, you don't have anything to be afraid of, do you? They can't accuse you of something you haven't done!"

"Oh, no?" Justin gave a bitter laugh. "If the person who stole the money gets away with it, I'll be suspected of this forever, whether I've done it or not. Don't you see that?"

Heather nodded. She understood it all too well.

"What did Betty want when you went into her office this morning?" she asked. "Did she talk about the stolen money?"

Justin shook his head. "Not directly. She told me she's trying to arrange it so that Bogart can be part my horse and partly be used as a school horse. Then I might be able to keep him."

"But that's good news, isn't it?"

Justin looked down. "Yeah, I suppose so, but the way she said it, I got the feeling she… she…"

"She what?"

"I got the feeling that she was telling me that I'll be able to keep Bogart even if I give back the money I've stolen. She didn't say it in so many words, but I'm pretty sure that's what she meant."

"So what did you say?"

"Nothing. I didn't know what to say, so I just mumbled something and left."

Justin looked up at Heather. Her heart started beating faster.

"Heather, it wasn't me who took the money. I'm innocent! Do you believe me?"

Heather looked him in the eye. Then she nodded slowly. "Yes, I believe you," she said, pushing away the little doubt that murmured in the back of her head.

Justin was almost his normal, cheerful self as they rode back together, but his high spirits quickly vanished when they got back to the stable. Betty and Kenny were waiting for them there. They looked serious and Heather felt a bad premonition in her stomach.

"I don't know how to say this." Betty looked kind of embarrassed. "There was a note on my desk when I got back a little while ago. At first I thought it was just a silly joke, but Kenny thinks I should take it seriously. And after I thought about it, I came to agree with him."

Heather looked at Betty without understanding. What was she talking about?

Betty took out a folded note from her pocket and read out loud.

Check Justin's grooming tool box. You'll find more than brushes there!

Heather gave a shocked glance at Justin. His face had stiffened, but his voice sounded pretty normal as he said, "This must be a very bad joke. I don't have anything but grooming tools in my box. Which I'm sure you saw for yourselves when you opened it.

"We haven't opened it." Betty looked him in the eye. "I didn't think it was right for me to check your grooming box without you being present. But I'd like you to open it now so that we can get to the bottom of this."

109

Justin and Heather tethered their horses outside the stable. Heather noticed that her hands were trembling.

Justin was already in the process of opening the box when Heather walked into the stable.

"Here! See for yourselves!" said Justin as he pulled away the lid. "There's nothing… what the…?"

It was silent as a grave in the room. At the bottom of the box, partially hidden by grooming brushes and other tools, were several twenty-dollar bills.

Justin looked up. His face had turned as white as a sheet. "That money is not mine," he said. "I have no idea how it got there. I didn't put it there, that's for sure!"

"I think you'd better come into my office so we can talk undisturbed," said Betty, and motioned for him to go with her.

Kenny stayed behind and picked up the money. It was a hundred and fifty dollars.

"Maybe now Betty will learn not to be so gullible," said Kenny, shaking his head. "I told her when that hoodlum came back to the stable, that 'once a scoundrel, always a scoundrel', but she wouldn't listen to me."

Heather didn't answer. She had a huge lump in her throat, and the tears were not far away. So it was true then. Justin was a thief. And she had actually believed him. Well, almost believed him, she thought ruefully! How could she have been so naïve?

Feeling depressed, she walked slowly outside to get Caliban. While she took the saddle off her horse, she recalled the conversation she'd had with Justin in the woods. He had seemed so honest and sincere. How could he lie straight to her face like that? She'd never trust him again, that's for sure!

Heather didn't know how long she had been standing there deep in her own thoughts, patting and stroking Caliban, when Angelica and Keisha came back.

Heather told them what had happened. But she couldn't bring herself to tell them how Justin had looked her straight in the eye and sworn that he was innocent. Thinking about it hurt too much.

Angelica understood how disappointed Heather was and didn't say much, but Keisha had no inhibitions. Of course she didn't know Justin from before either.

"Well, it was pretty logical that it had to be him," she said excitedly. "With all his money problems, who could blame him for falling for the temptation? But it was pretty stupid of him, because now he'll certainly be banished from the stable, and will probably not be able to keep Bogart."

"That'll make *you* happy, I guess!" said Angelica wryly. "Considering the way you've been driveling over that horse since you came here."

"That was mean!" said Keisha, looking insulted.

"But if Justin is forced to sell him, you'll be first in line, won't you?" Angelica wouldn't drop it.

"Of course! I'd be pretty stupid not to, wouldn't I?"

She didn't get any answers, because Betty came over to them just then, with a resigned expression on her face. Justin was nowhere to be seen.

"Would any of you have time to unsaddle Bogart and give him some hay and water?" Betty asked. "I told Justin to go home and think things through. And I promised that somebody would take care of Bogart so he wouldn't have to, the way things are."

"We'll see to Bogart," said Angelica quickly.

"Unfortunately, I have to go home," said Keisha, "but I'll be happy to take care of him in the morning. I assume Justin isn't coming tomorrow morning either?"

"Probably not," said Betty with a sigh. "So it would be nice if you'd take care of him in the morning. It's possible that Justin will come at some point. I hope so, for his sake."

"Why is that?" The girls looked quizzically at her.

Betty lowered her voice. "I'll expect you to keep this to yourselves," she said. "Justin still denies having anything to do with the stealing. After what happened today, it's difficult for me to believe him. I told him that I expect to get back the rest of my money at the latest by tomorrow. If not, I'll go to the police!"

Chapter 5

That evening, as Heather was biking home, her head was so filled with distressing thoughts that she almost ran into Justin when he suddenly jumped into the road in front of her. Heather stopped with hesitation. She didn't at all feel like talking to Justin right now. The disappointment at him having lied to her still burned inside of her.

"Heather, please, I have to talk to you!" Justin looked so pleadingly at her, she finally gave in.

"What do you want?" She looked at him. Was he about to tell her more lies?

"Somebody's setting me up," said Justin. "They're framing me!"

Heather gave him a skeptical look. "Framing you? What do you mean?"

"Somebody planted that money in my grooming box! Don't you see that?"

Heather shook her head. "Why would anybody do that?"

"I don't know!" Justin looked completely desperate. "I only know that I didn't put the money there. Think about it for a moment – it doesn't make any sense at all. Why would I steal four hundred and fifty dollars, take most of it with me, and then leave the rest in my own grooming box, where anyone could find it and trace it back to me? And who wrote the anonymous note and put it in Betty's office? I'd like to know that!"

At first Heather was skeptical, but what Justin was saying started sounding more and more logical as she listened to him.

It really was too stupid for him to have hidden money in his own grooming box. And if he had, wouldn't he have made sure nobody could see it, at least? Justin was not stupid.

When Heather lay in bed that night, she was wondering if she had made a huge mistake in promising to help Justin uncover who the real thief was. What if it was Justin after all?

"Stop it!" Heather told herself. "You've promised to help him, so you'd better believe that he's telling the truth."

She had believed Justin while she was talking to him, but now, lying here all alone not able to sleep, the doubt came sneaking back again. She brushed it resolutely away and started counting horses. They were jumping over a red and white hurdle. One horse, two horses, three... Oh darn, one of them escaped into the woods. Heather tried running after it, but her legs wouldn't move. The horse changed into a cloud that floated away. Heather slept, and dreamed about clouds, galloping horses and somebody who had sneaked into her room and tried to break open her piggy bank. But then Betty came and said she'd better stop this ridiculous dream or she would call the police...

Nobody expected to see Justin in the stable the next morning, but when Heather arrived he was there, waiting for her outside. They went inside together.

Keisha, who had been looking forward to caring for Bogart, was disappointed when she saw him. "What are you doing here?" she blurted out.

"Feeding my horse! Shouldn't I?" Justin gave her a look that didn't exactly spell friendliness.

"Yes, of course, but nobody thought you'd come today..." Keisha stopped, looking bewildered.

"And why shouldn't I? I haven't done anything to be ashamed of!"

114

Keisha hastily pulled away from the stall. Heather suppressed a smile. She couldn't help admiring Justin for being tough enough to come to the stable and act like nothing had happened. It couldn't be easy for him.

Heather went over to him. He gave her a quick smile.

"Have you talked to Betty?" she asked quietly.

Justin shook his head. "I'll do it as soon as I've given Bogart some food," he said. "I can't say I'm looking forward to it."

"Betty is all right," said Heather. "I think she'll listen to you. And she might even believe you."

They heard a car door slam outside, and the next moment Kenny came into the stable. When he discovered Justin, his face turned red. Clearly he had not expected to see him there. For a moment he stared aggressively at Justin, and then he turned and marched into Betty's office. He didn't stay long. A couple of minutes later, he came back out, no less agitated than before. He strode out the door, almost colliding with Angelica, and hissed something or other to her as he left. Next they heard the wheels in the gravel as he spun out of the drive.

"I might as well go into the lion's den and get it over with," said Justin as he walked toward the office.

Heather watched as he went, while crossing her fingers, hoping that Betty would at least listen to what he had to say.

Angelica came over to Heather just as Justin disappeared into the office.

"Is he going to confess and give the money back?"

Heather shook her head. "He doesn't have any money, because he's not the one who took it."

"How do you know?"

"Because it..." Heather didn't get any further, because Keisha practically attacked them with sensation-seeking excitement.

"Do you think he'll be able to pay back the money, or do you think he's spent it?"

115

"What are you talking about?" Heather was short and abrupt. Of course she knew what Keisha meant.

"Are you dense?" Keisha looked irritated. "Betty's money, of course! If she doesn't get it back, the police will come and take Justin away; she said so herself yesterday."

"No, she didn't! She said she would go to the police. There's no evidence that Justin took the money."

"Who else would it be? Of course it was Justin! I sure feel sorry for him if he can't give back the money."

"Well, that'll be up to Betty to decide, won't it?" Heather was really irritated now. "I don't understand why you're going on about this so much. It's not your money that was stolen."

"No, but what if I'm the next victim? None of us can feel safe as long as that crook is walking freely around here. You just wait and see who's right!"

Keisha tossed her head and marched away. They didn't see any more of her while they got Caliban and Crissy ready for a ride.

"Should I go and ask if she wants to come?" Heather looked at Angelica.

"No, if she wants to sulk why should we stop her? We can ask her tomorrow instead."

While Heather fastened the girdle, the office door was opened from the inside. Heather waited breathlessly. Would Justin come rushing out and go straight home, or... No, he and Betty came out together. Betty said a cheerful good morning to them and didn't look like anything special had happened.

"D'you want to come for a ride with Angelica and me?" asked Heather as Justin walked past her. He nodded and quickly went to get Bogart's saddle. Heather was dying with curiosity, but couldn't very well start asking Justin questions inside the stable. There were too many long ears listening in.

Keisha showed up just as they rode out from the farmyard. She didn't say anything, but was clearly resentful that she hadn't been invited to come along. She stood there, her back stiff with insult, as she watched them go.

"What did she say?" They were out by the woods now, and Heather couldn't help herself any longer. She had to find out now.

"What did who say?" Justin smiled teasingly, and Heather felt like strangling him.

"C'mon, don't stretch our patience any further. What did Betty say?"

Justin pretended not to want to answer now either, but when Angelica threatened to push him off the horse, he gave in.

While they rode along the trail, Justin told them how Betty at first had been convinced that he was the thief. But after a while she had started seeing that maybe it wasn't so clear-cut after all. Maybe it wasn't totally unreasonable that someone else could have put the money in the grooming box, as Justin insisted.

"I don't think she believes me one hundred percent," concluded Justin. "But at least she's willing to give me the benefit of the doubt, as she put it. I guess that's all I can ask."

"Hey, watch out!" he suddenly yelled at Heather. She had been so absorbed by his story that she hadn't paid attention to where she was going. When she looked up she saw a big, fat branch in front of her, and just barely managed to duck under it in time.

"Whew! Thanks for the warning!" She smiled at Justin.

"Don't mention it," he said with a chuckle. "I couldn't very well risk having you get a big bump and get even thicker in the head, you know."

"How rude!" Heather laughed and pinched off a pinecone that she threw at him. She missed by at least a yard.

"Gee, will you two cut it out?" said Angelica. "Stop being so childish and let's have some fun! Race you to the end of the field."

117

"Fine, but no cheating, giving yourself a head start like last time, do you hear?"

"Head start? Me?" Angelica rolled her eyes. Just then she reminded Heather so much of Caliban, the way he looked when he was trying to look innocent, that Heather burst out laughing.

"What are you laughing at?" asked Angelica suspiciously.

"Oh, nothing in particular. I'm just in a good mood, that's all. So, what's keeping you – are we racing, or are you waiting for moss to grow on your hooves?"

"Moss on your own hooves! Ready, set... go!"

Heather laughed in sheer delight as Caliban stretched into a full gallop on the soft ground. Right now life was exactly how it should be, and for a few precious moments all their worries were forgotten.

Chapter 6

During the next few days nothing special happened and the gossip dwindled down by itself. There wasn't really anything more to be said, even though most of them still looked suspiciously at Justin. He pretended not to see it. Keisha, who had been sulky for a few days, came around and had forgiven Heather and Angelica. The girls had some nice rides together. One day, while they were on their way home, they started talking about the riding camp later in the summer.

"It'll be so much fun!" said Angelica. "I can't wait."

Only it's too bad Justin didn't sign up, thought Heather. It would have been nice to have him along. After that ride a few days ago, Justin had withdrawn and kept mostly to himself. Heather was a little hurt by this. He was friendly and all whenever she ran into him in the stable, but he didn't want to ride with them. Maybe it was because Keisha was showing very clearly that she didn't really want to have anything to do with him. They hadn't made any further plans to find the real thief either. It almost looked like Justin was content to leave things as they were.

Heather was lost in thought, and didn't come to life until she suddenly heard Keisha say something about Bogart. She straightened up in the saddle. Angelica and Keisha were apparently done talking about the summer camp and had switched to a different topic.

"What did you say about Bogart?" Heather directed her question to Keisha.

"Oh, only that they're saying it's pretty certain now that

Justin has to sell him. Somebody heard Betty mention it to Kenny."

Poor Justin! If it was true, that would explain why he had been so quiet and withdrawn the last few days. Heather decided to talk to him as soon as she had a chance.

And the chance came sooner than she expected. As the girls turned into the farmyard, Justin came riding around the corner.

Heather waved to him. He nodded back, but didn't smile. It was clear that he was not in a particularly good mood.

While they dismounted, Heather said quietly, "Justin, do you have five minutes? I'd like to talk to you."

Justin shook his head abruptly. "Not now," he said. "I have somewhere to go, and I'd better get a move on. My ride took a little longer than I had planned. Can I talk to you tomorrow instead?"

"Okay," said Heather meekly. She wondered what all the rush was about. *Maybe I'll find out tomorrow*, she told herself.

Heather tried to hide her disappointment, but Angelica saw right through her.

"Are you sure he's worth it?" she said, sticking her head inside Caliban's stall.

"What do you mean?" Heather tried to look like she didn't know what her friend meant.

"What I mean is, that you are in love with Justin again! And I'm not at all sure that it's a good thing for you to be."

Heather felt her cheeks get warm. Was it that obvious?

Angelica gave her a serious look. "I think you would do well to think twice before you buy everything Justin tells you. And I'm sorry if you get mad at me for saying this, but you're my best friend and I don't want you to get hurt."

Heather looked at Angelica. She opened her mouth to say something, but to her shock and dismay she started crying instead. Angelica came into the stall with a bewildered look on her face.

"I'm sorry," she said. "I didn't mean to..."

Heather shook her head. "It's all right," she said between gasps. "I'm not mad or anything. It's just... I'm so confused! One day I believe him, the next day I don't know what to think. And you're right, I'm in love with him again, despite what he did last year and despite what he might have done now."

Heather sniffled as she wiped her eyes. She glanced over at Bogart's stall, worried that Justin would see her this way, crying like a baby. But Bogart was alone. Justin must have left already.

There was a clear snort from Caliban. He started pushing Heather with his muzzle to let her know how completely ignored he felt. Why was his master standing around crying and chatting about totally uninteresting things, while he, the most important thing in the world, didn't get as much as a look or a treat or anything? What was wrong with Heather?

"Oh Caliban, you're so wonderful," said Heather giving him a big hug. "What would I do without you?"

Caliban snorted again, but clearly this time he agreed. Finally she was talking some sense again!

Heather scratched him on the forehead as she wiped her eyes.

"What am I going to do?" she said miserably.

"Nothing at all!" stated Angelica firmly. "Behave exactly as you always have. I didn't mean for you to stop talking to Justin or anything, just to be a little careful and reserved. After all, we don't know if he's the thief or not, and he could very easily be innocent. I'm just not totally convinced that he is as truthful and nice as he appears. And I'll be the first to apologize if I'm wrong..."

"You know, you're starting to sound exactly like my mom!" said Heather with a chuckle. "She's been warning me too. I promise I'll listen to both of you, at least a little bit..."

"I'm glad somebody is having fun around here!" The accusatory voice made Heather give a start. Keisha was standing outside the stall waving her jacket around.

"Is something wrong?" Angelica looked quizzically at the jacket.

"Oh, only that someone has helped themselves to fifty bucks from the pocket of my jacket!"

"But what... who?" Heather and Angelica were both equally shocked.

"That's something Betty will have to figure out!" Keisha was furious. "I can't prove anything, but I think the answer is pretty obvious!"

"What do you mean?" Heather almost didn't dare to ask.

"What do I mean? I'll tell you what I mean." Keisha was so upset she was shaking. "I had the jacket with me on the ride. The money was in the pocket and the pocket was closed tight with a zipper. When we got back to the stable, I hung my jacket on the hook while I unsaddled and groomed Tinto. And now the money is gone! There haven't been a whole lot of people in the stable while we've been here, right?"

Heather shook her head. She saw where Keisha was going with this, and her heart sank.

"Justin was here, and then he suddenly took off like greased lightning. But it doesn't take long to unzip a pocket and run off with the contents. I'm willing to bet he did it! You just wait until Betty hears this!"

Keisha turned on her heel and strode off.

Heather watched her go while a feeling of helplessness filled her. The lump in her throat was back and the tears were not far away. She didn't want to admit it, but it looked like Angelica's warning had come at the right time.

Chapter 7

The next day, Heather didn't really feel like going to the stable, but she knew she must for Caliban's sake. She felt downright nauseated at the thought of meeting Justin. How could he have been so dumb as to steal money from Keisha? Didn't he realize that he would be the obvious suspect again? That was the very thought Heather had clung to as she was lying in bed not able to sleep last night.

Was it likely that Justin would have done such an unbelievably idiotic thing? Heather had a hard time believing it, but maybe it was possible, if he was desperate enough. Maybe he relied on them giving him the benefit of the doubt this time too.

Heather gave up her pondering as she leaned her bicycle against the stable wall. With a heavy heart she went into the stable. She felt a numbing relief when she saw that Bogart's stall was empty. Justin must have gone for a ride already.

She went into Caliban's stall and was greeted by his eager snorting. Caliban nudged his muzzle expectantly toward her pant pockets, hoping for a treat.

"You greedy beast!" Heather smiled and scratched his mane. "I have nothing in my pockets, but I'll give you some delicious hay, and maybe snatch a carrot for you if you're good!"

Caliban's head was nodding up and down as if he was telling her that he was definitely good. Heather scratched his forehead and laid her cheek against his nice, warm neck. No matter what happened, Caliban could always manage to get her in a better mood.

"… a scandal that he's not been arrested yet!"

Heather jumped. She hadn't heard the people entering the stable. But there, right inside the door, was Keisha and a couple of other girls. Keisha wasn't exactly saving her breath at the moment, hence her words could be heard all through the stable.

"I don't understand what Betty is thinking! That crook should have been banished from here a long time ago, then we wouldn't have to worry about the safety of our money. My mom was really upset when I told her what happened. I was supposed to spend the money on a gift for grandpa, so of course she had to give me more money. She didn't like that at all. She said she might have a talk with Betty. I hope she does, and then maybe we'll finally get rid of Justin! He doesn't deserve..."

She stopped abruptly as Betty came into the stable. Betty's voice was anything but friendly when she asked if the girls didn't have anything better to do than stand around backstabbing others. She didn't wait for any answers, but marched into her office, shutting the door with a bang.

Keisha stretched her tongue out to the closed door, but didn't have the guts to say anything more. Heather worried at first that she'd come over to Caliban's stall and start a new tirade about Justin, but fortunately she went straight into Tinto's stall. Heather gave a sigh of relief. She didn't blame Keisha for being mad about what had happened, but she didn't feel like talking to her about Justin right now.

An hour later Heather was in a much better mood. She was riding Caliban and enjoying the quiet around her. It had been overcast when she rode out, but now the sun was emerging from behind the clouds and flooding the landscape with a soft, golden light. Heather glanced over at Keisha and Angelica, who were riding beside her. Angelica smiled and winked at her and Heather smiled back. How lucky she was to have such a good and understanding friend as Angelica. When Keisha came and asked if she could come along with them, Heather had been tempted to say no, but she couldn't bring herself to do it. Angelica understood how she felt, and had pulled Keisha aside and whispered something to her. At first Keisha had looked irritated, but she nodded and shrugged her shoulders. Angelica had obviously warned her not to talk about Justin anymore, because Keisha hadn't mentioned him once during their ride, and Heather was grateful for that.

Where was Justin, by the way? What if they ran into him? Heather had mixed feelings, both wanting to and not wanting to talk to him. As if she had conjured him up with her thoughts, Bogart and Justin suddenly appeared in a clearing ahead of them. He reined in his horse, looking left and right as if he wasn't sure where to go. Heather held her breath as she wondered if he had seen her. It didn't look like he had, because he suddenly continued riding, and a moment later he and Bogart rode out of sight between the trees.

When they came back to the stable, Justin was already there. He was getting some hay for Bogart. Heather wondered if she should go over and talk to him, but decided not to. She was busy removing dirt and debris from Caliban's legs when the sound of his voice made her jump. She hadn't heard him coming. Taken by surprise, she looked up. "Did you say something?"

Justin nodded. His face looked serious and determined. "I have to talk to you. Could we meet tonight?"

Heather hesitated and Justin's expression hardened. "So you're like the rest of them," he said bitterly. "Thinking the worst about me. I guess I can't blame you." He shrugged his shoulders and turned to leave.

"Wait!" said Heather. He stopped. "Come over to my house around seven, then we'll..."

Before she could finish, a hysterical voice shouted, "My wallet! I accidentally left it on top of the oat bin, and now someone has taken all my money! I had forty dollars in my wallet and it's gone!"

A big commotion followed. One of the girls ran to get Betty in the middle of a riding lesson.

"Honestly, Lisa. Why would you leave your wallet on top of the oat bin?" Betty was shaking her head. "That's pretty irresponsible."

"Irresponsible? Me? You're the one who's irresponsible!" screamed Lisa furiously. "You're the one who's allowing the thief to walk around in the stable! This is your fault. Yours, and... his!"

She turned and pointed an accusing finger at Justin. "You... you, shameless thief! Give me back my money, or..."

Justin's face had turned dark red. 'I haven't touched your money!" he roared, so loud that several of the horses jumped and gave a startled neigh. They weren't used to such noise in the stable.

"Calm down everybody," said Betty firmly. "You're scaring the horses."

"I don't care!" Justin took a few threatening steps toward Lisa. "I'm sick and tired of being blamed for things I haven't done! Look here!" He turned out his pockets. "Not a penny! Go ahead and frisk me, if you want!"

"As if that would do any good!" Lisa stared furiously at him. "You've probably hidden the money already."
Justin clenched his fists and stared wildly at her for a moment, then he turned on his heel and ran toward the stable door.

"Justin! Wait!" Betty reached her arm out to stop him, but he brushed her away, and the next moment they watched him bike out of there as if he had a pack of wolves on his heels.

Heather waited for Justin in vain that evening. He didn't show up. She hadn't really expected him to either, after what happened. A whirr of thoughts filled her head as she went to bed. Guilty or not guilty? Everything seemed to point at the first, but something inside Heather refused to believe that Justin would do such idiotic things, especially since he was already under scrutiny. However, if it wasn't Justin, then who could it be? The day Keisha's money was taken there hadn't been very many people around during the brief time period in which the stealing could have taken place. Heather thought really hard for a while in order to remember who she had seen. But most of them had been at the stable for years, so it was pretty unlikely that one of them was the thief. Nobody had noticed anybody walking near the area where Keisha's jacket hung, or... ? Something stirred in Heather's memory, trying to get to the surface. It was something about... something about... no, she just couldn't put her finger on it, no matter how much she tried. Finally she fell asleep from sheer exhaustion.

Chapter 8

"Darn it!" Betty flung her arms out irritably. "I totally forgot that Amanda was supposed to come today to pick up Red Ron. That is so inconvenient right now!"

She glanced at her watch. "If I'd just thought of it yesterday, I could have called and rescheduled, but now it's too late. Oh well, I guess it'll work out somehow."

"Just tell us if there's something we can do," said Angelica. "I've been giving Lisa a hand, but she's done training now."

Betty gave her a grateful smile. "Would you be my assistant during a couple of riding lessons? Justin was scheduled to help me out, but he's obviously gone for the day, so I don't think we can count on him to be there."

"Huh, it was pretty brazen of him to come to the stable at all," commented Keisha. "I don't understand why you put up with him, Betty."

"I know it looks bad for him right now," said Betty seriously. "But as long as he says he's innocent, I can't very well throw him out. If it's proven that he's behind the stealing, then of course he can't continue coming here."

Betty scratched her head. "I don't know, maybe it's naive of me; I know that everything points at him, but I simply can't see Justin as a thief."

"Well, I sure can!" Keisha tossed her head. "I just know he's a thief, and besides he's almost a murderer too."

"That's enough!" said Betty annoyed. "Justin had nothing to do with the murder. And what he did afterwards happened because he was pressured by his own father. It was wrong of

128

him, but I'm sure he has regretted it every day since."

"I don't believe that for a second," said Keisha scornfully. "He's every bit as bad as his dad, I'm sure!" She turned abruptly and walked away.

"Gee, what's eating her?" asked Betty a little surprised.

"I don't know, I don't get it," said Heather. Keisha clearly had something against Justin.

"Hi there! You guys totally look like you've bitten into a sour apple."

"Kenny! You scared me!" Betty laughed as she put a hand on her throat. "I didn't hear you coming."

Kenny smiled and gave her a hug. Heather looked down. As always, she felt kind of dismayed when Kenny was around.

"I'm not staying," said Kenny. "Just thought I'd stop by for a second to see if everything's OK."

Betty shook her head. "No, everything's not OK," she said. "These thefts are going to be the end of me soon, and I'm being pressured left and right to banish Justin from the stable."

Here we go, thought Heather pessimistically. *Now Kenny will tell her what an idiot she's been not to throw Justin out a long time ago.* But to her astonishment, Kenny shook his head saying, "I think you're doing the right thing. Even if it looks like he's guilty, you have no proof. You'll just have to wait and see, and maybe the whole thing will solve itself."

Betty gave him a relieved smile. "Thank you!" she said. Then she looked at her watch. "I'd better get ready for lessons. And at eleven Amanda will be here to pick up Red Ron."

"Oh yeah, she's coming today." Kenny scratched his head. "I hope you'll go straight to the bank with the money," he said.

"That's impossible, you know that," said Betty. "But maybe you could stop by and take it for me?"

Kenny shook his head regretfully. "I wish I could," he said "But I'm on my way to Mexico to pick up some goods, and

I'll be gone for three or four days, maybe longer. Just make sure you lock up the money properly in your desk until you can go to the bank. And lock the door to the office too. Then the money should be safe."

"I'll do that," said Betty. "That is, if I can find the keys. I looked for them yesterday afternoon, but I couldn't find them anywhere."

Kenny laughed. "I'm surprised you can find anything at all in that mess. They're probably lying in between some papers and junk somewhere on your desk. But if you can't find them, don't you have an extra set of keys?"

Betty put her hand to her head. "I'm so stupid! Of course I do. They're at home, in the kitchen. I'll go and get them right away."

Kenny gave her a quick kiss goodbye, then he walked out, got in his car and drove off in a cloud of dust.

"Hey boy! You sure are a rowdy one!" Amanda laughed as she patted Red Ron on the flank. The horse snorted and tossed his head. He was clearly not too eager to be loaded into some scary horse trailer.

"If you wait two seconds, I'll be right back to help you. I'll just lock up this money in a safe place." Betty smiled and shook her head. "You really are crazy to be driving around with this much cash, Amanda. What if you're mugged some day?"

Amanda waved away Betty's words. "I'd like to see them try," she said. "I'm quite strong, you know. I can defend myself."

Betty hurried into the office. "Whoops!" she said, taking a step back as she almost collided with Justin, who was just on his way out of the stable with a wheelbarrow of wet straw.

Justin didn't say anything. Without looking right or left, he continued in the direction of the waste pile with his stinky load.

Two minutes later, Betty was back. "Oh, Keisha?" she called over her shoulder.

Keisha, who was on her way into the stable, stopped. "Yes?" she said quizzically.

"Would you be a doll and go and get a couple of carrots and some pellets, please? We'll have to tempt Red Ron with some treats, I think."

Keisha left and came back a moment later with the treats Betty had asked for. "Just let me know if you need anything else," she said. "I'll be in Tinto's stall, so just holler."

Betty went into the horse trailer and held a carrot out toward Red Ron. He took a few careful steps toward her. The whole horse was literally bristling with skepticism.

"Funny," whispered Angelica to Heather. "It's not like this is the first time he's been loaded into a trailer, so why all the fuss?"

"Maybe he understands that this time is different?" Heather thought for a second. "He might just feel that something isn't normal, even if he obviously can't know that he'll be moving away from here permanently."

Angelica nodded. "Horses are sensitive and intelligent animals, so it wouldn't surprise me if you were right."

Betty had managed to coach Red Ron partially up on the loading ramp. He stood there glancing suspiciously at the treat in front of him.

"Come, boy!" said Betty enticingly.

Red Ron took another careful step forward. Then suddenly he thrashed his head, gave a piercing neigh and jumped backwards off the ramp. Safely back on the ground, he started stomping his feet. His ears were bent straight back, as if he had just seen his worst enemy.

"Oh c'mon, Red Ron!" Betty's voice sounded resigned. "What's the matter with you today? You're not usually this difficult."

"Get one of the girls to stand inside the trailer with the treat," suggested Amanda. "Then you lead Red Ron around the trailer and up the ramp again. Don't let him stop this time. Be friendly, but firm. That's always my slogan when it comes to horses."

"I was just going to suggest the same thing myself," said Betty. The girls could tell she didn't really like having Amanda treat her like an amateur, but she didn't say anymore, just grabbed Red Ron's lead rope and took him with her around the trailer. When they came back to the loading ramp at a more vigorous tempo, Heather was standing inside the trailer ready with a carrot in her hand. Would it work this time? She held the carrot out toward him. It worked. It seemed like Red Ron could tell that Betty was not about to put up with any more nonsense, because he clambered up the ramp, snatched the carrot and started crunching it hungrily.

"Good boy," said Betty, patting his neck.

Ten minutes later they waved goodbye to the horse trailer as it left the farmyard.

"Red Ron will have a good life at Amanda's," said Betty with a sigh, "but I'm going to miss that rascal."

She glanced at her watch. "I have just enough time for a phone call before next lesson. I'll be right back."

"I don't think I'd like to be a riding instructor." Keisha, who had come out when Red Ron finally was being led into the horse transport, was looking at Betty as she rushed into her office. "It seems way too stressful."

"But exciting too," said Angelica. "I think..."

She didn't get to finish. Suddenly they heard a scream from the office. The next moment, Betty appeared in the doorway. "The money!" she moaned. "It's gone!"

Chapter 9

While Heather was grooming Caliban a while later, her thoughts were spinning wildly in her mind. Who could have taken the money? It didn't seem possible that it could be gone, but it was.

Betty had called the police and this time they said they would come. Heather hoped they would keep their word, because Betty was really upset.

"I can't afford to lose that much money," she said, pulling her hair so much it was sticking out in all directions. "This is a nightmare. The office door was locked, the desk was locked, and still the money is gone!"

"But how did you even come to check the desk?" Angelica asked.

Betty shrugged her shoulders. "I don't know," she said. "I just felt the need to make sure that the money was where I had put it. Probably because of all the unusual things that have happened around here lately. When I opened the drawer, I felt completely stupid for doing it, because obviously the money had to be there. And then it wasn't, after all. If it wasn't for the fact that I don't believe in supernatural things, I'd be tempted to think there's a ghost around here. If not... of course! Why didn't I think of that at once?" Betty put a hand to her head. "My keys! I couldn't find them, so I thought I had lost them somewhere. But what if somebody took them...?"

"Then they could just unlock the office, unlock the desk, take the money, and walk away with it!" Angelica looked excitedly at Betty. "And if you hadn't opened the drawer, the theft wouldn't have been discovered until later in the afternoon."

Betty nodded. "But as it was, I discovered it right after it happened. Somebody must have sneaked into the office during the half hour it took us to get Red Ron into the trailer."

"But everybody was outside watching him be loaded," commented Heather. "So who could have..."

"Justin!" said Keisha promptly. "He was inside the stable while I was working on Tinto, and though I can't swear to it, I'm pretty sure he walked past me and toward the office..."

Justin again! Heather had listened to Keisha with a numb feeling in her body. Could Justin really have done this?

Who needs money more desperately? said a voice inside her. With this much money, he wouldn't have to sell Bogart. If Justin had seen Betty lock up all that money, he might have been greatly tempted. Was he desperate enough? Surely he must understand that he would be suspected instantly.

Caliban tugged at Heather's sweater and she patted him distractedly.

But if it wasn't Justin, then who could it be? Heather kept asking herself repeatedly. While biking toward home, she was still pondering this question. She had taken a detour on her way home, in order to drop off her riding jacket at the dry cleaner.

While riding down a street in front of some condos, she couldn't help noticing a car parked in one of the driveways. It looked like Kenny's car. Heather knew that he had an apartment in this area, so this might be where he lived. No, of course not. How stupid of her, she thought. Kenny was on his way to Mexico and had his car with him... Her thoughts wandered back to the thefts. Justin had not been at the stable when Betty discovered that the money was gone, and he hadn't come back.

Keisha took this as proof that he was guilty. Why else would he disappear like that?

134

Heather was still lost in her own thoughts when she parked her bike outside her own house. She gave a start when she suddenly heard a voice behind her.

"Heather! I have to talk to you!"

Heather spun around. It was Justin. He looked seriously and pleadingly at her. Heather didn't know what to say or do. A part of her wanted to run right inside, slamming the door in his face. But a different part of her wanted to hear what Justin had to say. Her curiosity won the battle.

At first they just stood there looking perplexed at each other, both afraid to say anything. Finally Heather broke the silence.

"Where were you today? Why did you leave?"

Justin shrugged his shoulders dismally. "I just couldn't stand it anymore. All those accusing looks. Betty doesn't say anything, but I know what she's thinking. People are whispering behind my back, and if I come near them, they get quiet and look the other way. And that new girl, Keisha, is the worst. You'd think I had done something to her. She doesn't miss a single chance to dish dirt about me. I don't know what I can do to clear my name!"

Heather looked down, thinking about the five thousand dollars. Did Justin have that money at his home right now? Had he come over here to put her off with a lot of talk, so that she would speak for him to Betty? What was he actually after? Heather didn't understand it.

"If you're innocent, you don't have anything to worry about, do you?" she said quietly. "But you were there during the last theft, so I guess it's logical that you would be suspected."

"I wasn't there any more than anyone else, was I?" Justin looked aggressively at Heather. "That wallet was lying around in the stable all day, wasn't it? So anyone could have taken the money!"

"I'm not talking about Lisa's wallet! I'm talking about the last theft!"

"What do you mean?" Justin grabbed her arm so hard it made her whimper.

"Betty's money, of course!"

"What money?"

"The five thousand dollars that she got for Red Ron. It disappeared from her office while you were in the stable! Do you deny it?"

Justin wavered as if someone had hit him. All color left his face. Looking totally dazed, he leaned toward the wall. He tried to say something, but not a sound came out.

Heather just looked at him. No way could he act this well! Justin didn't know about this last robbery; Heather was one hundred percent sure of it! He was innocent!

"But if it wasn't Justin, then who could it be?" Heather looked at her mom. They were sitting in the living room and Heather had just told her mom everything that had happened the last few days.

"I can easily see why he would be suspected," said her mom thoughtfully. "Are you quite sure that he's telling you the truth?"

"Absolutely sure!" Heather looked straight at her mom. "You should have seen his reaction. He was white as a sheet and looked like he was in total shock."

"Hmmm, then it's most likely someone else who's behind the other thefts as well," said her mom. "It doesn't seem likely that there are several thieves around at the same time... Tell me again everything that happened. And include all the details you can remember from the different thefts."

Heather did as she was told. Afterward her mom was quiet for a while, thinking hard. Then she said, "What you've told me made me remember something. It's probably a long shot, but if I'm right..." She stopped as she jumped up.

"Stay here," she said. "I'm just going to check something." She took the cordless phone and went up to her bedroom.

It felt like an eternity to Heather before her mom came back. "I remembered correctly," she said, sitting back down on the couch. "It's not the most common name in the county, so I wonder..." She went silent, staring in front of herself. "I could still be wrong, but..."

"What are you talking about?" Heather was about to burst with impatience. "Could you please finish a sentence before I die of curiosity?"

Her mom smiled and patted Heather on the arm. "Sorry," she said. "I might be totally misleading you now, because it may just be a coincidence. We'll soon know if that's the case. But you see..."

The next morning, as Heather was riding her bike to the stable, she was still thinking about what her mom had told her. Could it really be? If so, it would explain a lot of things. But how could she prove it?

Heather threw her bike down outside the stable and hurried inside. Hardly anybody was there yet, but, fortunately, Angelica was. Heather rushed over to her. "I've got to talk to you," she said excitedly. "You won't believe what..."

Just then two younger girls were walking past them, and Heather stopped. It was too difficult to talk here in the stable where so many people could overhear what she was saying.

Half an hour later, Crissy and Caliban were saddled and ready, and the girls rode off together. For once, Heather wasn't able to relax and enjoy the ride. She had too many things to think about.

"Keisha will probably be offended that we took off without her," commented Angelica as they were approaching the woods.

"I can't help that," said Heather. "I had to talk to you alone."

"Well, talk away then! We won't get more privacy than this."

When Heather was done telling her, Angelica was speech-

137

less. She sat in silence on Crissy's back for a long while, then she said, "I think your mom's right. But how do we prove it?"

"I've thought about it." Heather bent down and patted Caliban on the neck. He nodded his head contentedly, looking like he enjoyed the ride. *Horses sure are lucky*, thought Heather. They never need to worry about anything or make difficult decisions.

"Maybe we could create a trap or something. But how?"

Angelica thought for a while. "I have an idea," she said. "With a little bit of luck, it might just work..."

She told Heather her plan.

Heather nodded in agreement. "It's worth a try," she said. "At least we have nothing to lose. And the sooner the better! The problem is, I don't have a penny on me right now."

"Me neither," said Angelica. "But who would know? We just have to sound convincing!"

Heather pulled out her cell phone. "I'm calling Justin," she said.

"What did you want to talk to me about?" Justin stood outside Caliban's stall, looking curiously at Heather.

She pulled him into the stall. "I'll explain later," she said. "You'll have to trust me. Just go into Bogart and do what you normally do."

Justin looked like he wanted to protest. Then he shrugged his shoulders and did as she said.

A while later, Keisha, Lisa and a couple of other girls walked past Crissy's stall. They stopped.

"I can't believe he has the gall to come here!" Lisa shook her head.

"I agree." Keisha sounded upset. "I really think it's time Betty does something about it, and tells him to stay away."

"She said today that she doesn't have any proof." Angelica said, shrugging her shoulders. "But if one more thing happens, she will turn Justin out of here immediately. She promised."

Angelica, who hadn't talked to Betty at all, was crossing her fingers behind her back.

As she had expected, it didn't take long before Keisha and the others had spread this news to everybody in the stable. *I only hope Betty doesn't get to hear what she has supposedly said*, thought Angelica.

Next, Heather started part two of their plan. "I'm going shopping for some new clothes after I'm done," she told anyone who cared to listen to her. "If I had known that Justin was going to be here today, I would have left the money at home. But, fortunately he doesn't know that I happen to have two hundred dollars in my coat pocket today, so I guess it'll be safe."

The stable was almost empty. Most of the people were out riding, either in the woods or in the ring. Justin was in the saddle room washing Bogart's bridle. Inside Caliban's stall sat Heather and Angelica as quiet as mice. If the thief was going to do anything, it would have to be now.

Then they heard footsteps in the hallway. Was it Justin coming back? No, the sound came from the opposite end of the stable. Carefully, Heather leaned forward to see better. There, on the hook on the wall, was her coat. And there, right next to it, stood a person looking around suspiciously. Then the person reached her hand into Heather's coat pocket, and...

"So! You couldn't resist the temptation, could you?"

Keisha spun around. Heather and Angelica stood up and glared accusingly at her.

"I, um, I..." Keisha couldn't find any good excuse for why she had her hand in Heather's pocket. The look on their faces said plainly that the game was over.

"That's not very nice, setting me up like that!" Keisha's eyes flashed with anger. Heather instinctively took a step back. She certainly hadn't expected this reaction.

139

"Not very nice?" Angelica looked at her in disbelief. "So, it's 'not very nice' of us to expose you, but it's perfectly okay for you to steal, is that what you mean?"

"I mean that I finally had the chance to get Justin thrown out of the stable for good. But now you two have ruined it all!"

Keisha was screaming the last part so loudly that Justin heard her and came running. Keisha pointed an accusing finger at him.

"I hate you!" she said.

Justin stopped dead, looking totally shocked. "But why? What have I ever done to you?"

"Done? You and that horrible father of yours... You killed... killed... my dad!"

Keisha suddenly covered her face in her hands and started sobbing loudly and uncontrollably.

Justin looked, if possible, even more confused. "What is she talking about? Is she saying... ?"

Heather nodded. "It was my mom who figured it out. I told her about all the things that have happened in the stable lately. We discussed who the thief could be if it wasn't you. That's when my mom suddenly remembered that Mr. Simmons, the man your father killed, had a daughter named Keisha. She called an old colleague to double check if it was true. Then she also found out that Keisha and her mom had changed their last names and moved in with Keisha's grandfather. After that we just put two and two together. Keisha had told us that her dad was killed in an accident, but that wasn't true."

"Your dad is an evil, wretched murderer!" Keisha straightened up. She had stopped crying. "And here you are, strutting about arrogantly in this stable, looking like you own the world! And to add insult to injury, you of all people have the very horse I want! It's not fair. My mom is a wreck because of what your dad did!"

"But you can't blame Justin for what his dad did!" Angelica stared at Keisha with anger and disbelief.

Heather saw in the crook of her eye how Justin shrank.

"I can too! He's just as bad as his father, because he helped him hide the murder, and that makes him an accomplice. I'll never forgive him! Never!"

"Do you mean to say that you came to this stable just so you could take revenge on Justin?"

Keisha shook her head. "No, that was a coincidence. But when you told me who he was, I figured that this was the best chance in the world to get him back for all the pain he and his dad caused my mom and me."

"So you stole money and framed Justin so that he would be blamed!"

Keisha nodded. She looked proud of herself. "The idea just occurred to me the day I fell off the horse and had to ride home. And I would have succeeded too, if it hadn't been for Heather's stupid mom! I should have changed my first name too, then nobody would have suspected me."

"But how *could* you take all that money from Betty? First four hundred and fifty dollars, and then five thousand dollars?" Angelica was furious. "After Betty has been so kind to you! How *could* you?"

"But I didn't!" Keisha looked Angelica straight in the eyes. "All I've done is to steal a couple of twenties from Lisa – and she has plenty of money anyway, and then I pretended that Justin had stolen money from me. Oh yes, and I took the four hundred and fifty dollars from Betty's moneybox. But that's just change, right? And I made sure that Betty got some of it back."

"The money you hid in my grooming tool box." Justin's eyes shot lightening bolts.

Keisha nodded. "Yes, but other than that, I haven't taken a penny from Betty! I have no idea who took the five thousand dollars. And that's the truth!" Heather and Angelica looked skeptically at her. Keisha glared stubbornly back.

141

"Believe what you want! I didn't take that money. But when it happened and Justin was blamed, I thought it was a total gift from heaven!"

It seemed clear that Keisha was telling the truth. Heather felt almost dizzy. She had thought that if she could just expose Keisha, the mystery would be solved. But apparently it wasn't that easy.

"But if it wasn't you; who was it then?"

Keisha tossed her head. She didn't look the slightest sorry for what she had done. "How would I know? Maybe it was him." She pointed at Justin. "I wouldn't be a bit surprised. That fool needs money in order to keep his precious horse. You can figure it out for yourselves. I'm not hanging around here any longer. I hope I won't see any of you again as long as I live!"

She turned around and started walking toward the door. Justin, who had been standing there like in a trance, came to life and ran after her. He grabbed her firmly by the arm.

"You are not going anywhere until you've talked to Betty and told her what you've done. You talk about me being so horrible, and maybe I am, but are you any better? I did what I did because I was scared of what my dad might do. You did it out of pure malice and vengefulness. It looks like you're proud of yourself, when you ought to be ashamed!"

Keisha's mouth started trembling, and for a moment it looked like she was going to cry. Then she straightened up and said in a cold voice. "Let go of me! I'll tell Betty everything before I go!"

As if on a cue, Betty showed up in the doorway. "What's going on here? She looked surprised, gazing from one to the other.

"Ask Keisha," said Justin quickly." She has quite a few things to tell you!"

Betty looked quizzically at Keisha.

"I don't want to say anything here. We can talk in there!"

Keisha tossed her head toward the office. Betty shrugged her shoulders, confused, and walked toward the office. Keisha threw one last hateful look at Justin as she followed behind Betty. Heather, Angelica and Justin looked at each other, none of them saying a word.

Chapter 10

"This is a real mystery," said Heather. A few days had gone by and they were no closer to an answer to who had taken the five thousand dollars from Betty's office.

"Just stop talking about it," said Angelica lazily. "We're not going to figure it out anyway. Let's just enjoy ourselves. By the way, don't you think we've rested long enough now? I'd like to keep riding."

They got up from the ground and onto their horses. Heather glanced over at Justin. He looked happier than she could remember him being in a long time. Even though he, in theory, could still be suspected of the last theft, nobody at this point seemed to believe that he was guilty. On the contrary, everybody in the stable felt bad about having been so thoroughly fooled by Keisha's mean trick. Now they made such an effort to be nice to Justin that he almost felt embarrassed by it, though it was a nice change from the whispering and hostile looks behind his back.

They rode in silence for a while. Heather relaxed and enjoyed the muted hoof beats against the soft ground. She bent forward, rumpling Caliban's mane. How lucky she was to have such a wonderful, pretty and good-natured horse, all her own! The sun had gone down and foreboding clouds promised rain, but Heather thought life was just great. The only cloud in her sky right now was that they hadn't been able to catch the thief who had gotten away with Betty's money.

Heather closed her eyes and felt how safe and nice it was to sit on Caliban's back. He carried her through the landscape and she didn't even have to look where she was going... Suddenly Heather remembered the branch that had almost swept her off Caliban's back only a week ago. Her eyes popped wide open, and she almost expected to see a big huge branch right in front of her. But there weren't any attacking branches in sight, so she quickly relaxed again.

When they got back from the ride, they saw Kenny's car parked outside the stable. Loud voices could be heard all the way out to the farmyard. Evidently Betty and Kenny were in the middle of a heated argument.

"I don't care what you think! Justin is innocent, and I'm willing to bet on it!" It was Betty's voice.

Heather, Angelica and Justin looked at each other. Justin's shoulders drooped. There could be no doubt what the argument was about.

"You are so naive, I can't believe it! Of course he took the money. He should have been kicked out of the stable. I regret being such a softy, telling you that you could wait and see."

"But it wasn't Justin who was behind the other thefts..."

The office door slammed shut, reducing the voices to muffled mumbling.

Heather looked at Justin. He shook his head and made a grimace.

"There's no end to this," he said bitterly. "I should have known that Kenny would insist that I have to be guilty regardless. I don't know why he dislikes me so much, but he's almost as bad as Keisha."

"One day before he left for Mexico, I was up on the hayloft cleaning. I was just sweeping up some dirt and junk over in the corner when he came up. I guess it must have startled him to see me there unexpectedly, but I don't see why he had to get so upset about it. He started yelling at me, asking what I was doing there, and told me never to set foot up there again. I tried to tell him I was actually doing Betty a favor, but he

145

wouldn't listen. Maybe he was just upset about something else and taking it out on me because he doesn't like me."

Justin shrugged his shoulders, then took Bogart into the stable. Heather followed him slowly. What Justin had just said made her think about something. Mechanically she started taking off Caliban's saddle and bridle, while her thoughts were dashing back and forth like spring foals.

Was it possible that... no, that's reaching too far... But she couldn't let it go. After she had given Caliban hay and brushed most of the dust off of him, she had made up her mind. She would talk to Betty. But when she peeked out the stable window, she saw Betty and Kenny get into his car and drive away. Heather shrugged her shoulders. It would have to wait then.

But maybe she could check something in the meantime, even if it did seem like an unlikely long shot.

I'm probably just letting my imagination get the best of me, she thought as she slipped upstairs to the loft. In the corner, Justin had said, but which corner? Heather looked around. On the left there were hay bales everywhere. It wouldn't make much sense to sweep the floor over there, as there was hardly any floor visible. But on the right there were only some tools and boxes. That's probably where Justin had been cleaning. Heather went into the corner and looked at the floor and the walls, examining them carefully. She saw nothing unusual. She walked all the way to the wall and suddenly felt one of the floorboards yield slightly under her foot. Quickly she moved to the side, crouched down and examined the floor. There was a knothole in the board. Heather stuck her finger into the hole. *Whoa, I hope there's not a big, hairy spider down there, ready to bite my finger*, she thought. *Or a rat!* But nothing bit her. Heather bent her finger and pulled. The floorboard made a creak and came loose easily, and Heather looked in disbelief at something lying in the hollow space underneath.

"Are you sure this is a good plan?" Angelica glanced up from the poster board she was writing on.

"As sure as I can be," Betty said, nodding satisfied. "Okay! That looks good. Just hang it over on the message board so everyone will see it."

Angelica did as she was told. Heather stepped up and read it out loud.

VOLUNTEERS NEEDED FOR LOFT CLEANING DUTY
To prevent any more injuries from protruding nails, splinters and loose items scattered on the hayloft, we'll have a big loft cleaning duty – tomorrow morning. Please bring a hammer and help us remove and secure dangerous nails, loose boards etc. I hope that many of you can come. Thanks for your help!
Betty

"Don't you have anything better to do?" said Kenny sarcastically when he arrived later and saw the poster. "Surely that could wait?"

Betty shook her head. "One of these days someone is going to get blood poisoning from one of those rusted nails up there. It's my responsibility to see that it doesn't happen."

Kenny shrugged his shoulders and left. Betty looked at him go. Then, with a thoughtful expression on her face, she went to get ready for a lesson.

The night was dark and quiet. It was warm and homey in the stable. The only sound was an occasional snort from the horses. Most of them were lying down in their stalls, sleeping peacefully. A couple of them were still standing up munching on leftover hay while snoozing in between. Suddenly the horses pricked up their ears. There was a creak from the door. Somebody was coming in. Was it morning already? But the light wasn't turned on. The horses relaxed again. A slight

147

squeak could be heard on the stairs up to the hayloft, then quiet footsteps across the floor. A flashlight came on, directing the light toward the corner of the room. The person holding the flashlight bent down toward the floor and pulled up a floorboard. A hand reached into the space under the floorboard and picked up something. At the same moment the light came on. The person whirled around, peering toward the unexpected light.

"Hi, Kenny! Are you looking for something?"

Kenny got on his feet, looking stunned as he met Betty's eyes.

"You didn't expect to meet people here, did you?" Betty's voice sounded sarcastic. "Maybe you came to get an early start on the loft cleaning?"

"Yes! I... I..." Kenny could tell how stupid it sounded and fell silent.

"I didn't want to believe that this could be true." Betty's eyes were almost black, as they flashed in anger toward Kenny's pitiful figure. "So I wanted to wait until I had proof before I called the police. And now I have it."

She took out her cell phone.

Kenny made a threatening step forward. "It'll be my word against yours. You know, I could just tell them that you're psychologically unbalanced and must have hidden the money yourself."

"And how will you explain the rest of the money?" Betty looked at him. "I counted it, and there's almost thirty thousand dollars in that package you're holding. You must have stolen from more people than me."

Kenny gave a crooked smile. "I don't call it stealing, I call it supplementary income," he said. "But I'll be nice to you. I'll go now, and leave your measly five thousand. Then you can try to convince the police that it wasn't stolen, if you want."

"I might have been able to live with you taking the money,"

said Betty quietly. "But not that you blamed Justin. Why did you do that?"

"Because it was so incredibly easy!" Kenny gave a satisfied grin. "Keisha played right into my hands when she started that ridiculous vendetta against Justin. Since he was already under scrutiny, suspected of theft, it was easy for me to borrow your keys and take the money. I already knew that Justin would be blamed for that too."

"You unbelievable dirt bag! To think that I was stupid enough to fall for a dirty scoundrel like you!" Betty was practically gritting her teeth in fury. "But I'm not about to let you get away with it. You belong in jail."

Kenny laughed scornfully. "You can't prove a thing," he said. "So just forget it."

"No proof, huh?" Betty triumphantly pulled a mini recorder out of her pocket. "I just happened to record every word you said!"

Kenny wasn't smiling anymore. "Give me that!" he said in a threatening voice.

"And why would I do that?" Betty looked defiantly at him.

"To keep me from knocking you over the head! It wasn't very smart of you to come here alone. I have all the cards in my hand, and I'm twice as strong as you, so you'd better hand it over."

"Do you really think I'm so stupid that I would come here alone?"

For a moment Kenny looked uncertain, then he laughed. "Nice try," he said. "But I'm not buying your little trick. Give me the recorder, or else..."

"Else what?"

Kenny spun around. Out from behind the stack of hay bales came Justin, Heather and Angelica. Kenny looked like he had landed in the middle of a bad dream. As it gradually became clear to him that the game really was over, he totally crumbled.

Epilogue

"I'm so glad this nightmare is finally over!" Heather patted Caliban on the neck as she looked at her friends. Justin sat on Bogart, smiling happily, and Angelica sat on Crissy's back, looking like a cat that had just been given a can of sardines. She had just been told that Anna wouldn't be picking up Crissy until after Christmas at the earliest, so naturally she was on cloud nine.

"It sure is wonderful to have my name cleared, finally." Justin stretched his arms up in the air in sheer joy. "I'm glad Kenny walked straight into our little trap. What a phony, making us all think he was going to Mexico!"

"He invented the trip to Mexico to make sure nobody would suspect him." Heather shook her head. "The worst part is, I actually saw his car! But since I knew he was out of town, I figured it was just some other car that looked the same."

"I talked to Betty before we left for our ride this morning," said Justin. "She said that Kenny will probably get several years in prison."

"Serves him right!" said Angelica with a little malice. "But I feel sorry for Betty. It must be quite a shock to discover that your boyfriend is a thief and a scoundrel!"

"She'll get over it," commented Heather. "She has her horses!"

Justin laughed. "Are you saying that four-legged friends are better than a two-legged boyfriend?"

Heather felt herself blush. "Not always!" she said as she glanced sideways at him.

Justin gave her a smile that made her melt inside.

"By the way, did you hear that Keisha has been banished from the stable until further notice?" said Angelica.

Heather and Justin both nodded. Betty had told them that if Keisha didn't regret what she did and ask Justin for forgiveness, she would not be allowed to come back to the stable.

"But it may not be an issue either way," Betty said. "I had a talk with Keisha's mom the other day. She was shocked at what Keisha did, and says she's considering taking Keisha with her and moving somewhere else."

"Well, it couldn't be far enough for me!" Justin rolled his eyes. "If she hadn't walked into that trap, I might have been the suspect for all eternity. I would probably have had to quit coming to the stable, and I would never have been able to use a different stable, where I would have to pay full price. Betty has been nice enough to let me keep Bogart here almost for free for the next few years, in exchange for me helping her with some of her lessons."

"How nicely everything is working out in the end!" Angelica smiled. "All that remains now is a tender kiss between the two of you, and everything will be perfect!"

This time Heather was not the only one who blushed.

"I think we'll wait on that until we don't have an audience," said Justin with a wink toward Heather. "Should we keep riding? We could race each other to the lake or something."

Heather nodded gratefully, collecting Caliban's reins and urging him into a gallop. He didn't need much persuasion, because he took off willingly. Heather felt the wind against her warm cheeks and smiled happily. Her horse was wonderful, the weather was wonderful, and when it came to her and Justin... well, time would tell. Right now Heather was happy with life just the way it was.